WORD GAMES

ALSO BY INES SAINT

WORD GAMES

ANGIE GOMEZ COZY MURDER MYSTERY, BOOK 2

INES SAINT

Book design by eBook Prep
www.ebookprep.com

June 2022
ISBN: 978-1-64457-251-1

ePublishing Works!
644 Shrewsbury Commons Ave
Ste 249
Shrewsbury PA 17361
United States of America
www.epublishingworks.com
Phone: 866-846-5123

ANGIE'S UNOFFICIAL ABRIDGED SPANISH AND PUERTO RICAN SPANISH/ENGLISH DICTIONARY

Abandonado: abandoned

Chiquita: little one (and used as an endearment)

Coquito: Puerto Rican holiday drink, with cream of coconut and rum.

Doña: Spanish prefix for matrons, Ladies, gentlewomen, etc.

fufú: hex, in Puerto Rico

hola: hello

mio: my or mine

muñeca: doll (and used as an endearment)

nada: nothing

nieta: granddaughter

querido: loved or beloved

ron cañita: distilled spirit made from sugarcane juice, referred to as "moonshine rum"

si: yes

tesoro: treasure

Tía: aunt

vela: candle

velar: to watch

ANGIE GOMEZ LAST WORDS (BOOK 1) RECAP

Angie's grandmother, Abuela Luci, reads Angie's fortune: "Many changes are coming your way, Angie. A stagnant matter will begin to move, aided by a change in your professional circumstances and a discovery about yourself."

Disbelieving but hopeful, Angie visits the new Major Crimes Unit Supervisor, Lieutenant Brian Mahoney, to pressure him to reopen her parents' decade-old murder cases. There's an instant spark between Angie and the Lieutenant. At the end of their meeting, Angie learns for the first time that a witness had come forward years ago to say that Angie's mom had been talking about wearing a valuable necklace the night she was killed. This witness bolstered detectives' theory about a burglary gone wrong. Angie doesn't believe it and is now determined to find out who this witness is since Lieutenant Mahoney can't reveal their identity.

As she is leaving the Sherriff's department, Angie finds out that her last client, the city's popular mayor, has been shot dead.

Two days later, the mayor's daughter, Brenda, shockingly asks Angie to restore her mother's face. Brenda was pleased with the bust Angie, an artist, was hired to sculpt the mayor and wants her mother's smile to be just as it was on that bust. Angie agrees to look at the mayor and think about it. While at the mortuary, Angie learns that when she is close to a corpse's head, she can hear the echo of their last words. Pappa, the funeral homeowner, and his grandson, Anthony, are present when this happens, and Angie screams. Startled, she tells them what happened. They test out Angie's ability with another corpse, one they happened to know in life. They believe her, and they agree to keep Angie's unique ability a secret. The mayor's last words were, "Bonnie *is* dead."

Angie works with Pappa and Anthony to determine if the mayor knows anyone named Bonnie. Through Pappa, Angie learns that the mayor, Tilly Sandberg, had a near-fatal accident years ago that made her reevaluate her life and repair her damaged relationship with her daughter, Brenda. Brenda accidentally provides the second clue; a baby picture of Tilly Sandberg at an orphanage with another baby named Bonnie. A distinctive birthmark is visible on Tilly's head.

Angie next discovers that Tilly no longer has this birthmark. Subtle questioning of the mayor's best friend, Tessa, leads Angie to make the first big break in the case: the mayor wasn't who she said she was. Like in a telenovela she and her grandmother once watched, the mayor, who everyone thought was Tilly Sandberg, was really Bonnie, her long-lost twin. Angie goes to the police with this discovery. She and Lieutenant Mahoney share a moment.

Tilly Sandberg's old and new hairstylists are now suspects because they may have noticed the missing birthmark and blackmailed her.

Angie catches the attention of a local journalist who wants to trade information about the mayor's case with information about Angie's parents' case. Angie finds out that the Air Force Office of Special Investigations took over her parents' case years ago and that she's been led on and lied to by people at the Sheriff's office. She also learns that there might be a clue to the witness who lied about Angie's mom at the home of Tilly Sandberg's old hairstylist, Lillian Carlson, who is now married to Neil Carlson, a wealthy and powerful man.

Angie and the journalist, Nalissa Jones, team up to infiltrate a fundraising gala held at the Carlson estate. They hope to learn more about Tilly Sandberg's old enemies and the false witness Angie is after. At the gala, Angie runs into Lieutenant Mahoney. She's furious with him, but he helps Angie and Nalissa avoid getting caught inside the Carlson home. Angie and Mahoney pretend to kiss, but the kiss becomes real. Nalissa is nearly caught anyway, but Pappa drives the 'getaway hearse' and hides her in a body bag.

Angie soon realizes that sleuthing isn't as easy as it seems. She must be ready to make enemies and mistakes and be more careful about whom she trusts. She is especially wary of Nalissa, who now knows the identity of the false witness in her parents' case and has disappeared. This leads to a dark moment where Angie and Abuela Luci have a heart-to-heart.

Angie is then called to the funeral home because Brenda has decided she forgives Bonnie, who is, in fact, her aunt, and wants to go through with the funeral. She wants to talk to Angie about changing Bonnie's appearance first. Angie is careful because she now wonders if Brenda might be the killer. She makes sure Pappa or Anthony will be there, but she and Brenda are alone when she arrives. Pappa and Anthony were called away to pick up a body.

Brenda and Angie talk, and Brenda leaves. Nalissa finally contacts Angie. She sends photographic evidence related to Angie's parents' case that also reveals something new about the mayor's best friend, Tessa. Tessa walks in then, sees Angie is onto her, and tries to kill her. While saving herself, Angie hears another corpse's last words: *"Remember. Shell."* Lieutenant Mahoney and the police show up soon after. Angie is confused because she sees Mahoney cares for her.

Angie, Anthony, and Pappa decide to offer discounts to murder victims' families so that Angie can get as close to as many victims as possible through her post-mortem reconstruction work, hear their last words, and help solve their murders. She also has new information on her parents' case to pursue.

ONE

"To attain the impossible, one must attempt the absurd."

MIGUEL DE CERVANTES SAAVEDRA,
DON QUIXOTE

"We're agreed, then?" Anthony looked us each in the eye in turn. Pappa and I both nodded without hesitation, excitement buzzing between us.

In the past two weeks, my life had changed in ways I had not yet begun to process. I had learned that, like many members of my dad's side of the family, I had a special gift. Mine was that I could hear a dead person's last words. Though I hadn't been sure how I felt about this at first, my so-called gift had led us to solve a high-profile murder. Now, instead of using my artistic skills to sculpt busts, I was working as a postmortem reconstruction specialist. This allowed me to get close enough to murder victims to hear their last words and then use this information to try and solve their cases. Pappa, the owner of Riverside Funeral Home, and his grandson Anthony, an erstwhile criminal defense lawyer, were now my partners. They were the first people I had allowed myself to trust in a long time.

Our misadventures also had us partnering with Nalissa Jones, a reporter now intent on solving my own parents' long-ago murders. I still wasn't sure how I felt about her or the new Major Crimes Supervisor at Montgomery County Sheriff's Office, Lieutenant Brian Mahoney. Both had helped me. Nalissa wanted a front-page story.

I wasn't sure what Mahoney wanted…

Anthony raised his hand and used his fingers to tick off the points of our new pact. "We'll attract murder victims to Riverside Funeral Home by offering discounts on services to their families, and then we'll use Angie's ability to hear a dead person's last words, Pappa's knowledge of dead bodies, and his connections in the community, and my criminal law background to help investigate each murder."

The word "murder" had us looking down at the corpse of Ronnie Martin, who was lying on the embalming table before us. "Our investigation will be different this time," I said with hope. "We know we can trust my ability, and we know what each of us brings to the table."

"Wait." Anthony glanced up with a sudden, arrested look in his eyes. "What if there's *more?*"

"*More*…what?" I prompted with a wave of my hand when his eyes glazed over.

"More gifts, as you call them," he explained with a shake of his head. "What if you can also feel a corpse's last feeling or smell the last thing they smelled?" He began to pace around the embalming table, eyeing Ronnie, clearly trying to come up with possible gifts. "Who knows? Maybe you can even see the last thing he saw."

Pappa's eyes widened. "Anthony! That's an excellent notion!" He gave me an encouraging nudge toward Ronnie.

My gaze darted from Pappa to Anthony before settling on Ronnie. "Just what do you expect me to do?"

"Start with his nose," Pappa said.

I eyed Ronnie. "Start with his nose," I repeated under my breath.

"Sniff inside it," Anthony instructed. "And then put your heart over his."

"Then gaze into his eyes and see if you get a vision. I'll prop his eyelids open." Pappa, who had been sitting on his work stool, went to stand by the body.

I stifled a sigh, leaned back, and tried to decide how best to approach Ronnie's nose. Their suggestions were perfectly sane after the week we'd had.

"Like this." Anthony leaned over the body and took a quick sniff into its nose. "See?" He tried to smile through his cringe. "Easy."

I rolled my eyes, but his gambit worked. I bent forward, sniffed the area around Ronnie's nose, and sprung right back up. "Nothing!" I managed to squeeze out.

"Now check his feelings like this." Pappa stood on his tiptoes, angled his heart to Ronnie's, and pressed his chest down until they were heart to heart. "See?"

My lips twitched at their commitment. I pressed my heart to Ronnie's to hide my grin and stayed there a long moment, making a solid effort to separate my feelings from anything new or foreign. I got up and shook my head. All I had felt was my own full heart.

"Take the eye caps out," Pappa instructed Anthony.

"Eye caps?" I repeated.

Anthony gave me a quick nod as he worked Ronnie's eyelids. "You weren't here for this last time, but we set the features before we embalm. We place these spiky eye caps—" he showed me what looked like spiky, flesh-colored contact lenses—"under the eyelids to keep them shut and give them their proper shape."

"A person's eyelids remain partially open in death because their muscles relax," Pappa further explained as he went to the front of Ronnie's head to keep his eyes open. "I was regretting that Ronnie hadn't donated his eyes, but now I see it was a good thing. We need to test the limits of your abilities. Now, look into his eyes, Angie."

This time, neither offered to demonstrate how to look a corpse in the eye. I bent forward with a shake of my head, opened my eyes wide, and gazed into Ronnie's.

At first, nothing. Then, the sound of metal slamming against metal. "Are we literally staring death in the eye now, Angie?"

I glanced sideways to see my dad's mom, Abuela Luci, standing at the open door. She was striving for humor, but her eyes were shadowed, and the edges of her mouth were tight. I recognized these as the signs of fear and worry that used to show up whenever my dad, a treasure hunter, would go on dangerous explorations. Abuela would never want to stop anyone from living their life, and she had learned that interfering could throw someone off their intended path, but it didn't mean she didn't feel. I wondered what I could do to take her mind off the fear.

"I thought I saw him wink at me," I explained as I straightened.

Intrigued, Abuela took a few steps forward and studied Ronnie with interest. "You think he winked at you? As if the two of you were in on a secret?"

"Mhm. Something like that."

Anthony gave me an exasperated look. "Uh, no. It was a spasm. Perfectly normal."

Pappa nodded. "And I was telling Angie how occasionally, people are declared dead even though they're still alive. She wanted to make sure that wasn't the case here."

Abuela nodded in understanding. "My third cousin twice removed, Monchito, got up during the middle of his wake and asked for a bottle of *ron cañita*. We gave it to him because we were too shocked to refuse, but his liver apparently couldn't handle much more because that last drop was what killed him."

I gave her a look. "You had moonshine rum at his funeral service?"

"Yes. We were going to drink a toast to him because that's what Monchito would have wanted." She paused for a beat. "So. Is he?"

"Is he what?" I asked.

"Dead-dead?"

"Oh. Yes. Very much so."

Abuela was now studying Ronnie with a disturbed look in her eyes. "What happened to him?"

"Apparent suicide," I said, suddenly wanting to know what she was thinking.

"It's possible," she said. "His aura is greatly troubled."

Pappa's head snapped back. "His aura? You mean to say dead people have auras, too?"

Abuela shook her head. Her gifts were reading auras and fortunes. "Only when their life force departs amid great emotional trauma. The turmoil leaves disturbing energy that can be seen and felt if you're attuned to these things. Did he leave a note or letter?"

"No." Pappa gazed at Abuela in awe before looking back down at Ronnie. "I wish I would have known all this sooner." I knew what he was thinking. Before me, someone might have told him, but he wouldn't have believed them.

"Why hadn't you told me this before?" I asked. "It's fascinating. You love to fascinate!"

"You never used to believe in my gifts. You pretended to, but I wasn't fooled." Her casual studied tone told me she knew better than to pry about why I'd had a sudden change of heart. Prying led to interfering, and one never knew where interfering could lead. I understood that now. Subtle machinations could change the course of a life.

Abuela shook off whatever she'd been thinking and reached back to pull an object from a deep leather bag slung over her shoulder.

Anthony whistled. "That's a nice machete."

I smiled. He was right. It was nice. It was painted like the Puerto Rican flag. The wooden handle had a white star in a blue triangle, and the long metal blade had three red and two alternating white stripes. "How'd you get me one so fast? You only mentioned it today." That statement had me glancing at the wall clock to see if it was, in fact, still "today." It was. Just barely.

"Manolo, an old friend who lives in the beautiful backwoods of Kentucky, makes them. Which is why I was away for six hours, and Albert couldn't reach me to tell me that his police scanner mentioned you were in a fix."

"Albert Witherspoon has a police scanner?" I asked next.

"His kids never visit him. He gets bored." She lifted a shoulder. I gave her a knowing look. Albert Witherspoon was also sweet on Abuela, liked to make her feel sorry for him, and knew one way into her heart was to bring her gossip.

"Hmph." I crossed my arms. "I bet he just loved calling you to tell you all about it without any thought to how late it was or how it would make you feel."

Abuela's eyes flashed, and I saw the tight grip she was wielding on her emotions slip. "And how do you think it made me feel, Angie, to learn that you were almost killed by Mayor Sandberg's murderer tonight?"

My heart sank, and I flew to her to hug her tight. Abuela held me close. At that moment, I was ready to walk away from the funeral home and any present—or future—investigations into murders, including my parents.

Abuela must've felt that her emotions were influencing my own because she stepped away and made a visible effort to get a hold of herself. "Tessa Baker," she said. "If you observed her closely enough, her tight little smiles and fists closed around her handbag gave away that she was easily and often offended, though she never confronted anyone. People like that collect a lifetime of petty grievances." Her jaw clenched. "And it was protecting that image of *mosquita muerta* that set her off."

Pappa raised an eyebrow in question, and she explained. "She was like a mosquito pretending to be dead, convincing everyone around her she was harmless, so no one suspected her of their bites."

"So, like a wolf in sheep's clothing?" Anthony put forward.

"No. Sharp teeth are easier to see. A stinger is well hidden. And if I ever see Tessa again, I will find her stinger, dislodge it painfully, so it never stings anyone again, and then I'll use it to stab her in the—"

"She didn't stand a chance with me, Abuela," I interrupted before she could get colorful. "I handled it. The police were super impressed." Nobody had come right out to say they were impressed with me, but they damn well should have been.

After an awkward silence where nobody backed me up on that, I gritted my teeth and reached for the machete. "I'll take that."

"Well, I'm proud of you, *mi niña*." Abuela's eyes glowed with pride, but she held the machete back. "I know you'll use it if you need to, but you must remember to keep it under your bed, with the handle where you can easily reach it."

Pappa studied it. "You know, I've always kept a baseball bat under my bed, but a machete can do more damage."

Anthony rolled his eyes. "Right. Especially if an intruder points a gun at you and asks you to hand it over."

I gave him a look. "You can sling the machete at the intruder and then duck."

Before Anthony could unleash his comeback, Abuela ordered us to hush. "I sense a restless soul in the vicinity," she explained.

Anthony, Pappa, and I all turned to look at Ronnie. I'm not sure what we expected him to do, but we were soon alerted that the restless soul was outside the door and not in the room. Nalissa stepped in with her palms out in front of her. "It's me, and she didn't sense my restless soul. She saw me out of the corner of her eye."

Abuela shrugged and gave me a wink. I responded with a weak smile. It took enormous restraint to keep myself from bombarding Nalissa with questions, but I had to wait for my grandmother to leave. Abuela must've sensed it because she thrust the machete into my hands and, in hushed tones, said, "I don't want you to stop living your life because of me, but I can't stop worrying, not after you were almost killed. But I've come up with a solution. You and I have a Zoom meeting with your cousin Wanda on Monday at nine in the morning. I'll meet you at your house, okay?"

It took me a moment to transition from remorse over having worried my grandmother to curiosity over the solution she had come up with. Cousin Wanda was the coolest. She was in her mid-thirties and looked like a cross between a Latina Marylin Monroe and an eighties-era Latina Madonna. Her candle magic and mediation store, *Vela Velar (vela* means candle, and *velar* means to watch), was its own little institution in Brooklyn. "Will our meeting with Wanda help you stop worrying?" I asked.

"We'll find out on Monday." She kissed my forehead. "Take care, Angelica." After whispering something to Nalissa, she left.

"What did she say?" Anthony asked her when Abuela left.

Nalissa shook her curly head. "She told me she thinks we're in the same boat—that our instincts are screaming one thing, but what feels right is something else altogether."

That made me pause. "What are your instincts screaming?"

Nalissa looked at the floor for a long moment. "To keep some of the things that I know to myself."

Pappa studied her. "And what feels right?"

She looked at him. "To share."

I set my new machete on the countertop, motioned for Anthony to close the door, and rolled a stool Nalissa's way. "Then, please, start sharing."

She treated me to a frank gaze. "I haven't decided what I'm going to do. My instincts and feelings are usually the same."

My jaw clenched, but I reminded myself that she had recently been mugged. As if to punctuate my thought, Nalissa plopped herself down on the stool and almost lost her balance. She was tough and always in motion, and I could hardly imagine her sitting still, let alone dropping down as if she'd had enough. Even her signature bright red lipstick had faded, and her short curls were lying flat.

"I'm sorry you were mugged and that your phone was stolen—" I began, but she held up a hand.

"Don't be. It's part of the job. And you've been through a lot, too. I heard what happened here. I'm sure we're both equally tired and wired."

"Right," I said with a frown. So wired that I hadn't realized I was tired until she mentioned it. Like a hyper but exhausted child who didn't want to miss anything by closing their eyes. I pinched the bridge of my nose. "Then why did you come here tonight?"

"To see how you were doing," she answered.

I removed my hand to study her. It was the truth, but not the whole truth.

Anthony crossed his arms. "You want the scoop about what happened here with Tessa Baker tonight."

He was right. She did.... And that gave me leverage. I went to squat before her. "Let's make a deal. I'll give you an exclusive interview about everything that happened here when Tessa tried to shoot me earlier tonight if you tell me everything you know about my parents' case."

She hesitated.

"We'll also give you an exclusive on our new case here…" Pappa gestured with his head toward Ronnie Martin. "If you always keep us in the loop. The moment you learn something new, you let us know."

I turned to smile up at Pappa.

"Another murder?" Nalissa now sounded wide awake.

"You don't have to look so happy about it," Anthony told her. "But we believe so."

"Why do you believe so?"

"That's all you're getting until you tell us what you know," Anthony replied.

Nalissa appeared to think about it for a while. Finally, she blew out a breath. "I can't believe I'm admitting this, but my brain is too scrambled to decide. It's pulling me in too many directions. Give me tonight to sleep on it, and we can meet tomorrow to talk."

"I'm being pulled in dozens of directions, too, but I know my priorities. It's time to decide yours," I insisted, but Pappa put his hands on my shoulders to stop me.

"She's right to want to recharge and be at her best, Angie. And she's not the only one who's tired. It's midnight, and we have a meeting with Ronnie's mom and fiancée tomorrow morning. Remember too that it's been a whirlwind week full of events for you." He squeezed my shoulder so I'd know what he was referring to.

I closed my eyes a moment. Whirlwind week indeed. I'm a Magical Gomez. I hear dead people's last words. I was almost murdered. *And I may be on the brink of solving my parents' murders.* I had Ronnie's case to think about, too.

Nalissa and I hauled ourselves up at the same time. "I'll stop by tomorrow after you meet with your new clients," she said, glancing over at Ronnie on her way out. Tired or not, I could see the wheels turning in her head. I suddenly knew we'd make a deal.

When she left, Anthony went to a drawer, brought out some index cards, and handed them to me. He met my questioning gaze and explained, "It would be helpful if you fill these out with bullet points about your parents' case. I only know what Pappa told me about it, but he only knows what he's read throughout the years. He didn't want to burden you with questions, but we need to know everything if we're going to help. Pappa's got a couple of old corkboards somewhere, and there's a small utility room upstairs where we can put them up. It'll be a good way to track everything we know about the cases we're investigating."

I reached for the index cards. "I can do that now," I began, but Pappa stopped me. "Let Anthony drive you home. For the sake of these cases, if not for your health, get some sleep, Angie. You'll see it'll all be clearer tomorrow."

I sighed. He was right. I had been running on emergency adrenaline fumes, and I was almost empty. Tomorrow all would be clearer. "Lock the door behind you," I reminded him as Anthony ushered me out. "People seem to keep waltzing in...."

TWO

"Grain by grain, the hen fills her crop."

SPANISH AND LATIN AMERICAN
PROVERB

L ast night, after I showered, my half-human, half-terrier-mix mutt, Tito, curled his warm little body next to my inert one in bed, and the next thing I knew, the sunlight was slanting down at me through my sheer white curtains.

My eyes blinked open, and the first thing I saw was the index cards on the desk in front of the window. Tito slid his head sideways under my hand, and I absentmindedly gave his right ear the good morning scratch he was demanding while I thought about organizing the facts of my parents' case into bullet points. Though my mind felt rested, and my thoughts were clear, I could not think in terms of bullet points. Pieces of information kept getting snagged or rolled into others.

My gaze shifted to a sketch of my parents I kept on the wall behind my desk. Its brushed, light gold frame complemented my sage green walls and picked up on my dad's bronze skin and my mom's coffee and cream coloring. It had taken me months to get the sketch right. The upward tilt on the left side of my mom's mouth when my dad amused her. The light in the corner of my dad's dark rum-colored eyes when he looked at her... The little details that eventually made it perfect came to me not when I was obsessively working on it but when I was busy with something else. *Give as much space and time to the fits and starts of the creative process as you give to the moments of fluidity, and you'll have genius flashes of insight,* my dad used to say. My mom explained it as the subconscious mind calmly sifting through everything, putting it together, and separating it until it was ready to present solutions.

I reached for my phone, which I had left charging on the nightstand beside my bed, and saw that Nalissa had texted me at six-thirty in the morning. It rankled that she had managed to get up before me. Her message told me she was already up and about and busy. Instead of meeting with us in the morning, as we'd agreed on last night, she was now saying she'd "pop by" at eleven-thirty a.m. on Monday. She didn't even ask if the new meeting time worked for us. Now I had to wait until tomorrow to find out what she knew... if she was willing to share at all.

Either she hadn't decided about partnering with us, or this was a power move to establish dominance in the relationship. Whatever her reason, she was calling the shots. *Ugh.* I threw my phone on the bed.

Tito abruptly stood and gave his fur a good shake. *"Come on, sleepyhead,"* his short barks seemed to shout out as he hopped off the bed. *"We're way behind on our morning rituals! Arf-arf!"* I followed his wagging tail to the bathroom sink, where I brushed my teeth, washed my face, and gave Tito his minty morning treat.

He was right. Getting out of bed at nine a.m. was unheard of for us. Everyone in my family who believed in reincarnation thought they had been an important or glamorous figure in another life. Not us. Tito and I were sure we had been peasants. We both kept peasant hours and would happily live off bread and cheese if we had to. If the bread was fried. Like an empanada. My stomach rumbled at the thought.

In that spirit, I pulled on a white peasant blouse with white tassels hanging from an open V-neck before making myself a buttery grilled cheese and filling Tito's water and food bowls. As I went about our comforting morning routine, my mind traveled back to the last time someone had asked me to detail my parents' case. Last week, Lieutenant Mahoney had wanted to know everything, even though he had all the facts in a file at his fingertips.

"Start at the beginning. How did a treasure hunter from Puerto Rico end up in Ohio?" he'd asked.

"You want me to start there?"

"Yes."

"Why?"

"Because in everyone's past, there's a crazy string of coincidences that brought them to where they are."

Though I now had reason to suspect Mahoney's true motives in getting the tale out of me, I could see his technique had been helpful. Threading the facts of the case into the story of my parents' life had helped me try out different links to see whether they fit.

I hadn't gotten anywhere with my speculations—there was still too much I didn't know—but vague ideas were now there, waiting to try on new facts as they come up to see if any of them take on a more specific form...

I thought of Tito's favorite show, Dateline. Years ago, I had written to its producers multiple times to get them to do a true-crime episode of my parents' case, hoping that someone would call in with a tip. They never replied. But Tito had gotten hooked on the show. His eyes followed the action as the host started first with the story and then with the crime.

My brain couldn't organize my parents' murders as index cards on a corkboard. It was too hard to decide what was or wasn't important enough. But I could write the story like a true-crime episode, and then Anthony or Pappa could extract bullet points from it. It would be easier than telling Mahoney because Anthony and Pappa were more of a blank slate. They had no case file of facts and leads, only old news articles and rumors. When possible, I could also try to remove myself from the story.

Eager to get started, I put down my sandwich, wiped my hands, and hurried to my room to fire up my laptop. I pretended I was in a dark, cozy room, being interviewed by a competent, compassionate host, and that someone watching my interview had the key to solving my parents' murders. As I typed, I could see how my subconscious mind had sifted through my options, like my mom used to say, and presented the insights my dad said guided him.

Back Story

My father, Julio Gomez, was an anthropologist with knowledge of the Taíno language once spoken by the indigenous people of

Puerto Rico. He had a knack for reading between the lines of historical documents and then making connections among the different things he'd read. His knowledge and skills led him to discover the whereabouts of *San Tomás*, a ship that sunk in the Bermuda Triangle in 1596. *San Tomás* was known to be carrying an obscene amount of gold, but my father believed it was also carrying what the Spaniards thought was the key to the Fountain of Youth. But locating and exploring shipwrecks takes a lot of money, and my dad had no choice but to take on a partner. He received several offers from deep-sea exploration companies but chose Tesorex because their goals aligned with his own.

My mother, Natalia Gomez, was an adaptive sonar and radar systems engineer with Tesorex, and she played an essential role in finding *San Tomás*. They fell in love at sea, the captain of the sea vessel they were on married them, and I was born in the middle of the Bermuda triangle, six weeks ahead of schedule and a few months before they located the shipwreck.

There were nineteen metric tons of gold and some amber found on the ship. The gold sparked a messy lawsuit about who owned it. After recouping costs, Tesorex meant for the rest of it to go to the people of various Caribbean islands and Mexico because it had been stolen from them. The Spanish government won the lawsuit, and the gold was all sent to Spain. All Tesorex had to show for their investment was amber stones and the advances they had made with adaptive radar, sonar, and signal processing.

What I Was Told

Sonrad Technologies, a contractor for Wright Patterson Air Force base here in Dayton, bought Tesorex because of their technological advances. Its CEO, Craig Fisher, offered my mom a job with an excellent salary and benefits.

The University of Dayton then offered my dad a position as a professor and researcher.

Everything lined up, and my parents felt that moving to Dayton would offer a young family more stability than treasure hunting.

Tesorex gave away some amber to crew members as souvenirs but lost track of most of it after assessing they preserved only gnat pupa. Complete insects or plant specimens were valuable in amber, gnat pupa not so much.

The Crime

Twelve years ago, my parents, Julio and Natalia Gomez, were murdered on their way to a reception at the Dayton Art Institute. It was the opening night of a roving exhibition of artifacts found on shipwrecks. My parents were to be the guests of honor. We lived nearby, it was a safe neighborhood where nothing ever happened, and they decided to walk. A dog got away from its owner and was heard barking before the sound of two gunshots reverberated through the alley. The dog owner, Aaron Parks, found his dog whimpering near my parents and trying to nudge them awake, and he immediately dialed 911. My mother's purse and my father's wallet were still on them. Mr. Parks admitted he was too afraid to check the network of alleys for the perpetrator, but he didn't hear footsteps. Detectives believe the dog interrupted the perpetrators and that it was a burglary gone wrong...

What I Believe

I believed some of the amber stones held important information and that my dad knew what that information was. Despite his reputation for taking risks, he was also responsible. If the information the stones held were powerful, he would've reported it to the United States Government. I believed this was why we ended up here in Dayton, Ohio. But something must have gone wrong. There was a saying in Puerto Rico that a secret between two people was no longer a secret. I think whatever they were working on was leaked to the wrong people, and my parents were murdered over it. Why did I believe all this?

- Because nothing found on a shipwreck from 1596 is historically unimportant enough to lose track of. Especially amber that had been selected for transport on a ship thought to contain secrets about the Fountain of Youth.
- My dad used to wear one of the ambers on a long, tough leather strip around his neck, tucked low under his shirt. The amber was round with black spots and looked like the sun. Other than my mom, only I knew of it because I was observant and nosy. When I asked him about it, he told me it was one of the souvenirs Tesorex gave away, and he wore it to remind himself how disappointing treasure hunting could be. When I asked why he hid it, he laughed and said he didn't want to be reminded about it all the time. But I believe he didn't fully trust anyone except my mom and kept one of the important amber pieces on him just in case. My dad's side of the family distrusts all institutions, and it would be just like him to keep it around his neck instead of placing it in a safety deposit box or fully trusting any government. Only I know the amber around his neck was taken the night of the murders, but even my grandmothers aren't sure they believe me. They never saw it, but they think it must have been a trinket that my dad simply stopped wearing at some point.

- My parents used to drive to work together, even though they worked for separate employers. When I asked them about it, they said that the University of Dayton and Sonrad were main contractors for the Air Force and that many of their employees worked at the base. But while it made sense for my mom to have worked onsite there because she was an engineer, my dad was an anthropologist. Why would he be at the base when he was supposed to be teaching?

Latest Developments

Lieutenant Mahoney recently told me that a witness came forward twelve years ago to say that my mom had been overheard bragging about a custom-made necklace she wore the night of the reception, one that my father had commissioned for her out of metals and stones he recovered from the first shipwreck he had salvaged. This gave credence to the "burglary gone wrong" motive. Detectives believed the perpetrators grabbed the necklace and were interrupted by the dog before they could take the purse and wallet, too. But I know for a fact this witness was lying. First, my mom never bragged about anything. Second, the "custom necklace" was a trinket of junk pieces that my dad made for my mom, it often fell apart, and it was a joke they often told.

Nalissa, a reporter with the *Dayton Gazette*, has a source who told her this "brag" took place at Lillian and Neil's tenth-anniversary party and that the witness stated they were sitting right next to my mom during dinner. Nalissa's source also told her that the Air Force Office of Special Investigations took over the investigation years ago. This confirmed my theory that the murders were not over a burglary gone wrong but were instead related to the amber stones and my parents' work for the government. I think the government believed me when I said my dad wore an amber around his neck, that it went missing that night, and that was why they took over the case.

Pictures of Carlson's tenth-anniversary party showed that Lillian Carlson was the person sitting next to my mom at the dinner and was likely the false witness. This was my first real lead in twelve years. And this was where I believed any investigation should start, by investigating Lillian Carlson and any link she might have to Sonrad or the government. What did she stand to gain from throwing investigators off course by telling them that a fake necklace was the real likely motive?

I sat back and reviewed what I had written. Anticipation filled me after rereading that last sentence, and I could no longer wait to get started. I hit compose on my email account before realizing I didn't have Anthony or Pappa's email addresses.

I shrugged, printed two copies, and placed them in my messenger bag before slinging it over my shoulder.

Tito must've sensed I was doing something important because he waited until I was done before he began a frenzy of barks and scratches at the front door. Guilty that I had made him wait so long, I hurried to click his leash on his collar.

I hadn't stepped out the front door before Tito nearly pulled my arm out of it's socket and started a new round of mad barks. His arch-nemesis, the designer Shih-Poo from down the street, was strutting down the sidewalk with her nosy owner. A few other neighbors were casually hanging out and chatting right in front of our house while discreetly glancing at my front door from time to time.

I shut the door and leaned against it. Word must've gotten around that I had helped solve Mayor Sandberg's murder and had almost gotten killed.

I tiptoed over to peek out the front window. A white Altima with tinted windows drove by. Tito put his paws on the window to loudly question its presence. We were on the last block of McDaniel Street, which ended at Hathorne School Condos, and like a gossipy *Doña*, Tito knew every car and person on the street and quickly wondered about new ones.

Changing course, I took Tito to do his morning business in the backyard. This wasn't part of his usual morning routine, and there was a whole lot of sniffing, investigating, and rotating before he found the perfect spot.

I filled a treat toy up with peanut butter for him before I left, and he raised his tail and twirled it round and round to let me know he forgave me for not walking him. Licking all the peanut butter out from every inner crevice was his equivalent to five happy hours.

I pulled up the garage door and got in my dad's car, but it wouldn't start. I banged my head on the steering wheel when I realized I was out of gas. Hadn't I put gas in the tank a week ago? I had barely driven it.

Willing to go to great lengths to avoid my nosy but caring neighbors, I got out, crossed the alley behind my house, jumped the iron fence surrounding Mrs. Goetz's backyard, snuck up the side, and jaywalked (or jay-ran) across North Main Street, where I caught a glimpse of the same white Altima that had been on my street a few minutes before.

With the danger of nosy neighbors behind me, I strolled down Best, a quiet street where it was doubtful anyone would recognize me, while I caught my breath. The sound of a speeding car was so out of place that I glanced back, surprised, in time to see the white Altima screeching around the corner and speeding up the street.

It took me a moment to react. My first thought was, *why is a car zooming up this quiet street?* Then, *Oh, yeah! Nalissa and I were seen sneaking around the Carlson home, and she was mugged! Maybe they're after me now!* I spun around, trying to think of the pitfalls of every route available to me before taking off on a run down the sideyard of the nearest house. I didn't stop to look back as I jumped fences and zigzagged across yards and streets like a spaz while listening for the sound of a speeding car. I had sprinted across two streets before I heard it again, and by then, I was crouching behind a dumpster. It occurred to me that my messenger bag held two copies of printouts naming names. In hindsight, that had not been smart.

I looked out. One more house and its yard and fence, and I'd be on Riverside, on the opposite side of the road from the funeral home. I didn't feel the presence behind me until I was hauled off the fence from behind. One of the tassels on my shirt got caught on the chain-link fence and tore away. I screamed as loud as I could and flailed my arms and legs every which way.

I was dropped so suddenly that I almost fell face-first onto the grass. The person behind me steadied me, but their touch made me whip around, ready to go berserk again.

THREE

"He who doesn't like the broth is sure to get two
    cups of it."

SPANISH AND LATIN AMERICAN
PROVERB

And there was Brian Mahoney, standing in front of a fountain that featured a huge, flaming red-crested rooster on top. I hated roosters. Almost as badly as I wanted to hate Brian Mahoney. But my pulse was already speeding up at his nearness. I looked down and clenched my fists. This strange attraction to him was beyond my control. I would never have thought it possible.

"Why are you following in a white Altima with tinted windows?" I demanded.

His eyes widened, and he took off to where he could look up and down the street. "I'm not following you," he called behind him.

"This is my house. I was getting into my car when I saw you sneaking across my yard. And I don't see a white Altima."

I sighed. Last night, he'd said he lived close by, which was why he'd gotten to the funeral home first. *Of all the backyards, in all the neighborhoods, in all the world, I walked into his.* "Why do you have a giant rooster fountain in your backyard?"

"It was here when I moved, but I'll admit it called to me. And it's not that big."

"Yes, it is. And of course, it called to you. Roosters are aggressive harassers."

"I don't know a thing about roosters, but Mr. Leni told me the original owner believed it would guard her against trouble." Mr. Leni was an amateur historian who knew the history of every house in the district. "It doesn't appear to be working for me, though." He gave me a pointed look. "What are you up to now, Angie?"

I clutched my messenger bag with the printout closer to me. "I'm on my way to the funeral home."

He glanced at my bag before raising an eyebrow. "This isn't the typical way to the funeral home."

I shrugged. "Nosy neighbors were waiting for me outside my house this morning, and I decided to stay off the main roads."

"Why did you accuse me of following you in a white Altima with tinted windows?"

Note to self: be less specific and forthcoming around Brian Mahoney. And don't clutch your bag to you. It looks suspicious. "When you attacked me, I assumed you were the last person I saw."

He frowned. "And the last person you saw was following you in a white Altima with tinted windows? Did you get a good look at them?"

"No. Like I said, the windows were tinted. And they were probably just driving down the street. Your attack is what made me think I had been followed."

His bright blue eyes bore into mine. "It wasn't an attack. You were trespassing, and I stopped you. Now can you please stop trying to pick an argument with me and tell me what made you think you were being followed?" He looked genuinely concerned, and it confused me.

Questions and doubts about him that had been flurrying in the back of my mind suddenly blew forward and left me cold. "Nalissa was mugged at her house the night you saw us at the Carlson's. Her phone was stolen. I'm being extra vigilant, distrustful, and suspicious because I was with her that night. Which you know since you were the only person to recognize her."

He stared hard at me. A muscle jumped in his jaw. But he didn't say a thing. It was almost like he was counting to ten. Or twenty. Finally, when the storm in his eyes calmed, he simply said, "I'm glad you're being careful, Angie." He broke eye contact to reach into his back pocket. He dug out his wallet, took out a card, stepped forward with an intense look in his eyes, and dropped it into my messenger bag before patting it as if to tell me he'd noticed I was protecting it. My impulse was to scold him not to touch my property, but I bit it back. It would be better to end our latest interlude.

It would be best if I could end them all.

Not wanting to go around his house to where the white Altima could still be waiting, I turned to the chain-link fence and braced myself to climb it and jump over to the other side in front of him. "There's a gate to your left," he noted. I nodded without looking at him and left that way.

Halfway across Riverside, when I saw no cars were coming, I dug my phone out of my bag and Face-Timed my cousin Wanda. I needed to stop running into Lieutenant Mahoney, and magic, now that I believed in it, might be my best chance.

A weight lifted off my shoulders when I saw her dark-brown eyes light up as brightly as the big, fluorescent green bow tied atop her black shoulder-length curls. "Angie! *Muñeca*! How are you?" Before I could answer, she pouted and said, "Only so-so? What can Wanda do?" with her comforting and charming lisp.

"Help me get rid of someone?" I asked.

She gave me a solemn nod. "I know you, and you wouldn't ask unless it was necessary." Her eyes shifted left and right, and she moved closer to the camera. "I know a woman, a vigilante—"

My eyes widened. "No! Not that kind of getting rid of. I mean, I want someone out of my life. Safely and soundly out of my life. Like, still living their own life. Just out of mine."

She perked up. "Oh! That's more easily done. My vigilante has strict standards about her magic. Me, not so much. Do you still have the colored candles I got you when you were five?"

"I do." My mom had hidden them, but I'd found them a few years ago. *Most five-year-olds get boxes of colored crayons for their birthday. Mine gets colored candles and is encouraged to play with fire;* Mom had said as she boxed them up.

"Is the twilight blue half an inch tall still?"

I'd never used any of them, so, "Yes."

"Well, you're in luck because tonight is the first night of the waning moon." She clapped her hands and shifted forward again. "Use something narrow and pointy, like a pin or a pimple popper, and carve the name of the person you want to draw away from you from the bottom of the candle to the top. Meditate carefully on it, focusing on a vision of this person leaving your sphere for as long as you can. Then stare into the flame and chant, '*of so and so set me free, if the universe so agrees.*' But substitute *so and so* for the name of the person you are trying to keep away from you. It works every time." She smiled but then quickly put a finger to her mouth and frowned. "Unless it is the universe's will for *so and so* to be close to you. Questions?"

I walked the sidewalk alongside the cemetery and went through her instructions in my mind, but before I could think of any questions, an alert for another FaceTime call popped up. My eyes widened. Holy Google alert. "Abuela Nydia is on the other line."

"Your mom's mom?" Wanda crossed herself, blew me a kiss, and disconnected.

I hit answer and looked into my mother's mother's penetrating, dark-amber eyes. "*Hola, Abuela!*" I greeted her cheerfully. Abuela and I had a longstanding agreement that I'd speak to her in Spanish, and she'd speak to me in English so we could each practice the language we spoke least in our daily lives.

"Don't *Hola Abuela* me, Angelica. Is it true you almost got shot while working as a cosmetician at a funeral home?"

"*Sí.*"

She threw her hands in the air. "Is that all you have to say?"

"¡Me voy a ganar $400 por hora, Abuela! Y trabajar en una funeraria no es peligroso, solo esta vez por esta señora desajustada que mato a la alcaldesa. ¿No lo leíste?"

"You're going to earn $400 an hour! Finally, your degree will be put to good use, and you will have security, Angelica! It's all about security." She banged her hand on a table at each of those words. "Your mother would agree. And yes, I did read all about the mayor and the deranged woman who murdered her, and I also agree that working in a funeral home doesn't sound like it would normally be dangerous." She paused. "Maybe cut your hair, so it doesn't get in your face while you're bending down and working. I assume you need to bend down. Get it cut like mine." She ran her hands through her layered, perfectly dyed, light-brown-and-caramel highlighted hair. "And don't take on any more murder victims in the future, to be safe. Does the funeral have home proper ventilation systems and hazmat disposal protocols?"

"Si." To the ventilation and hazmat. Not to the avoiding murder victims and cutting my hair.

"Really? And what do you know about proper ventilation and hazmat disposal protocols? Never mind. I have an important phone call to make. We'll talk later. I love you, Chiquita." She blew me a kiss.

"Abuela, don't you dare—" But she hung up, and I was sure she was about to call Pappa to question him about his ventilation and hazmat protocols. Good thing the Georgian building was already before me. I ran down the long driveway to the back.

Anthony opened the door just as the phone rang. I held my hands out and shouted, "If the area code is 787, don't pick up!" to Pappa, who was about to answer the phone.

"Why am I getting a call from Puerto Rico?" he asked, looking down at the Caller ID.

"It's my Abuela Nydia. She has questions about ventilation and hazmat disposal. You don't want to—"

"Nonsense. I'll be happy to answer them." He hung up fifteen minutes later, looking like he sucked on a lemon. "Your grandmother knows her stuff. Good thing I do, too. More than she." The conversation had been contentious, to say the least.

"I'm sorry." I gave him a sympathetic look.

"She did warn you," Anthony said, looking amused. "Good thing Mrs. Martin and Chelsea Hampshire called to say they were running late." He looked up at the clock. It was close to ten. "Can we expect visits or calls from your grandfathers next, or can we pick up where we left off last night?"

"Never met my grandfathers," I tossed back as I walked to the embalming table. "Men in my family die young. Weak hearts on one side, poor decisions on the other." I ignored the look they exchanged.

"So? Anything?" Anthony asked.

It took me a moment to remember I had been trying to feel and see and smell whatever Ronald had in his final moments when Abuela Luci interrupted us last night. I glanced at the clock before looking back down at Ronnie. His mother and fiancée would be here soon, grieving and wanting answers. There would be time enough to tell them about the white Altima. "No. And don't even mention taste because I think we can rule out all other senses at this point."

"One is enough. We'll have to use our other skills to see what else we can figure out," Pappa said consolingly before straightening.

"I'll take you through the evidence against murder." He swept an arm toward Ronnie. "Our subject is six feet two inches tall and two hundred and forty pounds. A person would have to be extraordinarily strong to stage a suicide by hanging. They'd have to strangle him first, immobilize him somehow, and then lift him. There would be defensive wounds if he were strangled, and there are none, and if he were immobilized, it would be by a blow to the head to render him unconscious or by using some drug. There are no contusions on the head, though, and no injection sites. If he was given drugs to incapacitate him, it seems he would have drunk or inhaled them. Anne says nothing was found at the scene, not even a glass of water. Without a toxicology report, which wasn't ordered, we'll have no way of knowing."

"Why wasn't it ordered if the mom believes he may have been murdered?" I asked.

"The body would need to be taken to the coroner's office, and the dad doesn't want to prolong all this. Post-mortem toxicology tests are also complicated and can take weeks to complete. It would be helpful in the long run, but we wouldn't get answers right away. I told Anne she might try anyway, but she doesn't want to go against her husband's wishes."

"Did she seem submissive to you?" I asked Anthony, not understanding why the mom wouldn't plow ahead, no matter what, if she had doubts.

He shook his head. "No. But they're both grieving. She may regret it later, but we also can't push her."

I let out a sigh because it suddenly did make sense. As close as I was to both my grandmothers, I could never convince them about my theories regarding my parents, and I'd given up trying because I didn't want to hurt them any further.

Anthony considered Ronnie. "The fact that he spoke and said something seemingly meaningful is a strike against him being incapacitated with drugs."

Pappa tilted his head to the side. "Unless they used some sort of muscle relaxant?" He shook his head. "But that would likely affect his throat, too, and he wouldn't have been able to speak."

"And wouldn't there be bruises or finger marks on the neck if he was strangled?" I asked as I studied Ronnie's neck.

Anthony shook his head. "Only about half of strangulation victims ever show any marks on their necks.

Another new interesting fact to store. I turned to Pappa again. "Is there *anything* that points to murder, other than interesting last words and what his mom and fiancée believe?"

"Well, the cause of death was strangulation. In hanging cases, it means the neck didn't break, usually because the fall is short, which it was. It wasn't difficult for me and Anthony to get him down when we picked him up." My eyes widened. There was still a lot I didn't know about the funeral business. I hadn't even suspected that it was their job to bring the body down. "Although still difficult," Pappa continued. "I can see a strong person, or persons, lifting him that distance if Ronnie was at least somewhat incapacitated and not struggling. And although staging something like this is difficult, it's not impossible, and the outcome is an open-and-shut case that keeps officials from investigating further."

"So basically, the only evidence pointing to murder is that he *could* have been incapacitated by drinking or inhaling drugs and that someone *could* have lifted him, and that it *could* be a smart choice for covering a murder because it keeps officials from investigating further, which we've seen." It wasn't much. "Maybe his last words were to himself." I shrugged before looking up. "No matter what, it would still help to know who Shell is."

Pappa agreed. "I asked Anne Martin to bring pictures of Ronnie's close family and friends to display during the wake, and we can try to gently and kindly find out their names as she reminisces. I also want to see who looks like they had the strength to lift him, and while I make conversation about the pictures, also learn if anyone is named Shell."

After a long moment, Anthony turned to me. "Did Ronnie croak his last words, or did he sound strangled? Because the first time you told us what you heard, you said that Ronnie spoke in a strangled voice, but you described it as croaking the second time. Maybe you should listen again. You said it helped with Mayor Sandberg's investigation."

He was right. So far, the first and only time I heard Ronnie say, *"Remember. Shell."* was while I was escaping a murderer wielding a gun. My attention had been elsewhere. The second time I got close to his head, Abuela had burst in and distracted me. I stepped forward to put my head near Ronnie's and stayed there a long time, listening repeatedly. Finally, I got up. "Both croaked and strangled, and as if he didn't mean to pause between the two words but couldn't help it because he couldn't get the words out. Like…" I looked to Pappa for moral guidance. It felt wrong to imitate a recently deceased person's last words, but how else could I explain?

Pappa granted permission by gesturing magnanimously with his hand. "It's for the case and the greater good."

I repeated, *"Remember Shell,"* exactly like it sounded to me. "It's like he was telling someone, or maybe even himself, to remember this Shell person." My eyes widened. "Wait. Didn't you say his fiancée's name was Chelsea?"

Anthony nodded in confirmation and waited for me to continue.

I tried to say "*Chel*" while constricting my breath, and it sounded like I was croaking out *Shell*. "What if he was saying, *Chel?*" I suggested.

Anthony and Pappa tried it, too, and soon we were all repeating it, trying it out with different breath restrictions. Each time, it came out, "Shell."

A throat clearing sound made us look at the stairs that led up to the funeral home's main floor. Two women were standing on the landing staring down at us.

We exchanged wide-eyed, horrified glances before Pappa scurried up to greet them. "Let's all sit in the reception room," he said. "It should be empty, and there's more room there than in the arrangement room where we met yesterday." Anthony followed, and I made up the rear, shaking my head at the absurdity of it all. Thank goodness we hadn't been saying, *Remember Shell*. If either of the two women were the murderer, they'd be wondering how we knew his last words...

"We really need to start locking doors," Anthony whispered out of the side of his mouth.

FOUR

The funeral home's reception room was an elegant, peaceful, cozy room. Beige walls, dark paneling, cream and gold brocade furniture, and hardwood floors covered with pastel Persian rugs. Money was tight, but the upkeep of the public rooms was a priority. It was the same with the five viewing rooms.

After introductions and condolences were made, and motives for their visit and choosing us explained, we dragged three armchairs over to where Ronnie's mom and fiancée had settled on a sofa and prompted Anne Martin to tell us her story, but it was Chelsea who began.

"He was acting strange and distracted lately as if he had something on his mind." Her lips trembled, and she pressed them together before continuing. "He seemed…unhappy. And withdrawn. But…he wouldn't share what was wrong." She stroked her engagement ring absent-mindedly until her gaze met mine. "I know that points to someone who is, or who was,

49

thinking about taking his—" she paused and tried to take a breath but couldn't manage it. One hand went to her chest.

This was grief. I knew it well. And it was challenging to witness. Pappa pressed her free hand gently, and she looked down and began to sob as if she'd been given permission.

Ronnie's mom, Anne, put her arm around Chelsea's shoulder, closed her eyes, and breathed in and out a few times before opening them again. "He was going through something tough that he wouldn't share, but he was *not* suicidal. He was the star of the Dayton Dutch Dragons," she said, naming our League Two USL soccer team in Dayton, "And he was about to move up to Fort Lauderdale CF. He was excited about that. And relieved. Whatever was going on with him, he was looking forward to the future." She looked at me. "We were hoping you could see something…." She took in a shaky breath and looked down as if to get a hold of herself again. "We're desperate. Too many people noticed he had been depressed. Even my husband—his dad, accepts that Ronnie took his own life. You're my last-ditch effort." She looked at me. "We're hoping you see something. Anything. Something that less-observant people have missed."

I chose my words as carefully as I could. "I understand, and I'll do my best. But we may need to ask you some difficult questions and talk to other people who knew him as if we were real detectives—which we know we're not. But that's how we figured things out last time," I explained and looked to Pappa and Anthony for support. They nodded their agreement. "It was the whole of what we figured out together that made my one observation meaningful. Does that make sense?" I spoke to Mrs. Martin, but both women looked up and nodded gratefully.

Anthony took over, and where I was awkwardly sincere, and Pappa had the perfect touch in the face of despair, he was efficient in a way that focused our attention and their emotions on our current shared goal of figuring out what happened to Ronnie Martin.

While he spoke and asked a few questions, I studied both women to see if there were any subtle changes in their expressions. He dug for a motive for anyone wanting to kill Ronnie, but both women seemed at a loss.

"No life insurance, for example?" Anthony gently pressed.

Anne thought about it. "The team has one on each player for career-ending injuries or accidental death, but no life insurance that I know of."

"After we got engaged, he tried to get life insurance, but it was crazy expensive because he's a professional athlete in a contact sport," Chelsea added. "I told him to forget about it."

"Who saw him alive last?" Anthony asked next.

"My husband, Dan, was with him earlier in the evening," Anne answered as she wiped her eyes with a tissue.

"Does he have an alibi for later that night?"

"The coroner determined the time of death to be two to four in the morning, and Dan was sleeping next to me."

"Are you sure?"

"I'm a light sleeper. I always have been, and my profession now demands it, as I often get emergency calls in the night," she explained.

Anthony tilted his head. "What do you do for a living?"

"I'm a large-animal veterinarian specializing in livestock."

"I'm sorry, should I have been calling you Dr. Martin?" he asked.

She lifted a shoulder. "Mrs. Martin is what my Ronnie's friends have always called me, and it's fine." Her voice cracked, and she looked down, her breathing fast and shallow now, and we averted our eyes to give her a moment. She blew her nose, took a shaky breath, and gestured for us to continue.

"Who were Ronnie's closest friends?" Anthony gently asked.

"Lately, just Luke Wilson, his roommate," Chelsea said, fumbling for her phone. She didn't strike me as a fumbler in general. "I'll send you his contact information right now."

Pappa and I exchanged a discreet glance. She wanted us to talk to Luke.

"Have you asked Luke Wilson what he thinks about all this?" Anthony asked.

"I tried, but he was almost catatonic," Anne explained.

Anthony glanced at Chelsea. "Were any of his teammates upset that he was moving up a league that you know of?"

Chelsea took a steadying breath. "Ronnie mentioned that Sheldon Douglas, the head coach, was put out by it."

Sheldon! *Shell.* It took a monumental effort not to whip my head around to stare at Pappa and Anthony. "Put out?" Pappa repeated, and I marveled at how nonchalant he sounded.

Chelsea's shoulders slumped. "That's all Ronnie said. He didn't elaborate, but he didn't seem concerned. He only mentioned it after I forced him to tell me about his day. We used to tell each other everything, but I had to pull every word out of him."

"Did Sheldon and Ronnie get along in general?" I asked.

Chelsea shook her head. "They got along as coach and player…
but Ronnie didn't want a personal relationship with him." She
looked down at her hands, and I felt there was something she
wasn't telling us.

"We'd like to talk to the players, too. How can we reach them?"
Anthony asked.

"They practice every day from seven-thirty am until Sheldon says
they're done."

Anthony wrote that down before glancing back up. "And what do
you and Dan Martin do for a living?" he asked, looking first at
Chelsea. Both women seemed taken aback. Anthony explained,
"We already know Mrs. Martin is a livestock vet, but we don't
know what anyone else does. It's part of putting everything
together. Someone might have wanted to hurt you through
Ronnie."

Both seemed skeptical that their careers had anything to do with
Ronnie's death, but they answered. "I'm an aesthetic nurse at
Birch Med Spa," Chelsea said, naming a highly reviewed local
day spa known for providing nonsurgical beauty solutions at
reasonable prices.

"And Dan's a sportswriter," Anne spoke next.

Anthony wrote that down, too, before gently asking. "Who found
Ronnie?"

"Luke," Anne answered with a furtive glance at Chelsea.

Chelsea took a deep breath and let it out before giving Anne's
hand a half-hearted squeeze. "Anne doesn't want to upset me,"
Chelsea explained when she saw us looking between the two of
them. "Luke and I don't get along. He and Ronnie met at Wright
State three years ago, during their sophomore year. Ronnie

befriended Luke because Luke wanted to be a sportswriter, like Dan. Ronnie thought he could help him. But Luke is always talking about his feelings and encouraging others to overshare. He's always trying to get Ronnie to talk about our relationship. I find it irritating."

"Do you think he may have had something to do with Ronnie's death?" I asked.

Chelsea shook her head. "Luke had just gotten back from a conference in Columbus with a few other students when he found Ronnie. The timeline checks out that he called the police, and us, the moment he got home and found Ronnie. And I can't think of a motive for him." Chelsea blew her nose.

We ended the interview shortly after because Mayor Sandberg's private memorial service was set to begin in half an hour. With all the hoopla surrounding Mayor Sandberg being an impostor twin and sweet old Tessa Baker being the murderer and almost killing me, too, only her daughter Brenda, Brenda's husband, Pappa, and their pastor would be attending the service and funeral.

Anne asked to speak to Pappa alone for a moment. She had the pictures Pappa had asked for and a few requests. Chelsea went out to the car, and Anthony began regaling me with the details about a state-of-the-art security system he was planning to install to keep Pappa and me safe. My lips twitched at his enthusiasm. One new thing to add to my storage of knowledge about Anthony: he was a tech geek.

When Anne left, Pappa strode over to us, and I tried not to show how happy it made me to see him standing straighter. I was glad Anthony was upgrading their security. A new purpose in life would mean nothing if Pappa wasn't safe. "Nobody in the pictures was called Shell." He handed over the pictures Anne had given to him. "His father is a good five inches shorter than him, but he's muscular where Ronnie was lean. If Ronnie was incapacitated and lifted after he was dead, the dad looks like he could be strong enough," Pappa observed with a shrug.

I looked through the pictures and stopped at one of Ronnie and his soccer team. "His teammates and coach all look strong, too, which makes sense. They must work out a lot."

"Did she want to discuss funeral plans?" Anthony asked after he looked through the pictures, too.

"That—and she wanted to weigh in on what Chelsea said about Ronnie's roommate, Luke. According to Anne Martin, Chelsea was pushing Ronnie to move in with her, and Ronnie was using Luke as an excuse not to, saying that he didn't want to leave Luke paying all the rent. The truth was that Ronnie wasn't ready for that kind of commitment."

I frowned. "If he wasn't ready to move in with her, why did he ask her to marry him? If you're ready for the biggest step of all, you'd be ready to move in. Was it because of his religious beliefs?"

Pappa shook his head. "I asked because of the service, and he wasn't religious."

"I'm curious about Dan Martin. I understand he accepts death's cause, but why not approve a toxicology report to help his wife move on?" Anthony asked.

I agreed. "It's a reasonable request. But I think we should focus our attention on Chelsea or Sheldon because of *Shell*. There's a lot to sift through, but the one piece of information we have that no one else does is *Remember Shell*."

Anthony was thinking along the same lines. "I'll call Luke Wilson and push him to talk to us today. He was Ronnie's closest friend, and if Ronnie used Luke as an excuse for not moving in with Chelsea, he would likely confide in him about troubles with his coach or his girlfriend. We can find out more about *both* Shells. Tomorrow, we can show up at his old team's practice. It doesn't sound like Dan Martin would be willing to talk to us anyway."

"And I'll hold the fort down here, of course, but I need you to get started on Ronnie soon, Angie. His service and funeral are this Wednesday," Pappa reminded me.

I gave him a firm nod. "I'd also like to speak with Brenda Mumford. I want to ask her what she knows about her real mom's relationship with Lillian Carlson. Tilly Sandberg clearly had something on Lillian, and my instinct is that Brenda will help me with my parents' case if she can. I know today's not a good day, but if you can gauge how she's doing overall, I can get an idea of when to approach her."

"All right then." Anthony clapped his hands together. "Let's get moving. I'll call Luke Wilson."

Anthony went to make the call while Pappa and I discussed Ronnie's cosmetic needs. Anthony was soon returning to us, a satisfied expression on his face. "He said he can meet us today at one at his and Ronnie's apartment." He looked at his watch. "Nalissa should be here soon, giving enough time to interrogate her."

"About that," I began, and Anthony hit me with a weary look. "She texted me early this morning to say things had come up, and she'd pop by tomorrow at eleven-thirty a.m."

Anthony let out a disgusted grunt. "Power move."

"Or—maybe she needed more time to think about it," Pappa suggested.

Anthony wasn't having it. "Nope. She wants to call the shots."

"That was exactly my thought. But that means she's willing to cooperate. She just wants the upper hand." I gave Anthony an imploring look. "We need to let her think she does because I don't want any more delays like this. No hardball tomorrow. Don't use words like *interrogate*."

He took a deep breath and gave a half-eye roll before agreeing. "Fine. We'll try it your way."

"And there's more." I hesitated because I should have told them as soon as I walked into the preparation room. "This morning, I was followed on my way here."

"You were followed! And you're only telling us now!" Pappa exclaimed.

"I was going to tell you as soon as I walked in, but then my grandmother called you, and we got sidetracked."

Anthony sighed deeply. "Explain."

I went over everything, from writing up the particulars of my parents' case to the moment I looked outside and first saw the Altima to ending up in Lieutenant Mahoney's yard and how it had to be related to the pictures me and Nalissa took.

Anthony ran both hands through his hair. "You were carrying a printout with your suspicions of your parents' case on you as you were being followed by someone who would likely love to know said suspicions?"

"Yes. In hindsight…" I began and then let the thought drop with a shrug. Anthony held his hand out, I dug into my messenger bag, and I gave them each a copy.

"Two copies," Anthony muttered and shook his head.

"I don't like this," Pappa spoke as he read. "First Nalissa and now you."

"It means we're rattling someone, and the one thing Nalissa and I have in common is that we were both at the Carlson's, and we are both looking into my parents' case. I also don't think they meant to hurt me. I think whoever it is wants me to know I'm being watched. They want to frighten me into backing off. But I don't think they would risk hurting me. Everyone knows I've been looking into my parents' murders for years. Too many people would wonder if anything happened to me."

Anthony looked up. "I think you're right. I don't think they would risk anything happening to you that would bring widespread speculation to the case again, and it's true that the only thing you have in common is that you were both at the Carlson's. But unless Pappa was followed, only Mahoney knew."

"Mahoney's also the one who told me about the witness in the first place. I don't know what to think about him." I gave my head a slight shake. "Lillian Carlson, on the other hand…being a false witness and obstructing an investigation is a huge risk. Lillian had to have a strong motive to agree to it, but other than asking Brenda if Tilly ever gossiped about Lillian, I don't know where to start with her. I want to learn everything about her, and asking her friends seems risky. They might tip her off. I think I should start following her. All day if it's necessary."

Pappa frowned. "Following her for hours at a time is risky. What car would you even use? And how would you find time for anything else? I'm not worried you'll let us down with Ronnie, but don't you teach at an after-school program? And at a senior center? Don't stop living your life, Angie."

"Mondays, I have the after-school program, and I'm with the seniors on Wednesday evenings. Hopefully, Lillian has events or plans with Neil in the evenings, or they will stay in. I want to see what she does all day. And I'll rent a car. A black Ford Taurus. Nothing more inconspicuous than that." I smirked because it was the car Mahoney drove.

The gold in Anthony's hazel eyes suddenly blazed to life. "Why not use a tracking device on Lillian's car instead of following her?"

"A tracking device," I repeated. "That sounds illegal. I don't want you to get into more trouble, Anthony."

"We won't get in trouble if no one can track it back to us…."

FIVE

"Many people go looking for wool and come back shorn."

MIGUEL CERVANTES SAAVEDRA,
DON QUIXOTE

"Why do you have a magnetized, coin-sized tracking device, a fake license plate for your motorcycle, and a burner phone for the device?" I asked an hour later. We were hiding out at a park Lillian needed to pass if she left her house. If she did, we'd follow on Anthony's motorcycle, disguised by helmets and light, oversized windbreakers. My hair was pinned up under the helmet.

Pappa stayed behind, eager to organize the bullet points for both cases on the corkboards. He also wanted to work on setting up the little room he and Anthony had deemed our command center while tending to his regular duties.

"The Cleveland case that got me in trouble. I had backup plans to my backup plans," Anthony explained.

I didn't want to hurt his feelings or remind him of bad times, but… "*Plan A* was to break into a government building?"

"I had a key. They only called it breaking and entering because I wasn't supposed to have it. But I only had it because my ex gave it to me. Plausible deniability. See?"

"Plausible deniability of what? You might get disbarred, and you were charged."

"I was charged but not convicted. And justice, *true* justice, was served. Again, I wish I had been less zealous and more careful, but I don't regret it."

I put my helmet to my head and tried to think. "I don't like your idea of placing the tracking device under the car when she stops somewhere. It leaves us at the mercy of unknown surroundings. Motorcycles zigzag. It's not something anyone would find suspicious. I think we should be on the lookout for a good moment to zig in behind her, I can lean in and put the magnet underneath the wheel case, and then you can zag back out."

"You think that putting your hand near a moving tire is a better plan than waiting to see where she parks? Do you even know what car she drives and how low the wheel case might be?"

"She drives an Audi R8 Spyder. And it's Oakwood. The top speed here is thirty-five miles per hour. How dangerous can it be? Or are you worried about your maneuvering skills?" He didn't have time to answer because a car drove past, and we looked up to see it was Lillian in a newish, grey Grand Jeep Cherokee Laredo. "Let's go!" I whispered in his ear, pressing his legs as if he were a horse.

Anthony flashed me a look before pulling down his visor. "Your impatience is understandable, but it will keep you from being inconspicuous. Take it from me." He revved up his motorcycle just as Lillian hit her left-hand turn signal. "We're going to have to wait for her to park somewhere. And remember we're meeting Luke at two. Following Lillian might be a bust today, but at least we tried."

He was right about all of it. I held my breath as Lillian turned right onto an inner road. For some reason, I was expecting her to turn onto Far Hills, the town's main street. "It's going to be harder to follow her if she's taking an inner route, isn't it?" I asked.

"We'll see." Anthony squeezed my hand and pulled out. It was as if he sensed my anxiousness and understood it but knew it wasn't helpful. Maybe he had felt this way before breaking into this ex-boyfriend's office. He had gotten caught, so I appreciated his gentle warnings.

It was, in fact, easier to follow Lillian through the maze of winding inner roads of beautiful West Oakwood. We could wait to see where she was turning, under cover of mature trees, without being seen, and follow her while looking like a couple on a leisurely Sunday ride.

Anthony leaned forward to look to the left. "She's still at the stop sign, texting."

"I never would've pictured her in a Jeep—even if it is top of the line. Not flashy enough for her."

He turned his head. "If she usually drives an Audi R8 Spyder, she may take out this Jeep when she wants to be incognito. This is the car we need to track."

I smiled. "Good thing you know how the criminal mind works." After another moment, I asked. "What kind of motorcycle is this, anyway?"

He turned to look at me fully. *"Are you serious?"*

"Um. Uh-huh."

"It's a Harley."

I glared at him. "I'm a *car* person, not a *motorcycle* person."

"Everyone knows a Harley."

"That's not—" I stopped, surprised when Lillian turned left and began to round Hills and Dales Metropark, heading south. "The Fishers live near here...or rather, Craig Fisher. They separated last year, and she's the one who moved out of the family home. It's why I haven't heard from them in a while. They're going through a lot."

It took a moment for Anthony to react. "Fisher as in Craig Fisher? The CEO of Sonrad, where your mom worked, right?"

"Right. Good memory, seeing as you only skimmed the printout," I answered distractedly, still not believing that could be where she was heading. "Jessica and Craig Fisher have both been kind to me."

Anthony followed until Lillian turned left again. "Definitely the Fishers." I swallowed hard and tried not to let any new emotions get the better of me. "The good news is that the house is on a wooded lot, and the nearest neighbor won't see us unless they're out for a stroll or drive. The bad news is it's a long driveway."

We looked around. Woods everywhere. "Leave me here," I said, swinging off the Harley before he could stop me. "Drive around and circle back until you see me again. I'll keep my helmet on and go through the woods."

"Angie—"

"I heard you before, Anthony, and you were right. My feelings are bound to spell trouble. But I've got them in hand now. I don't want to mess this up. I *can't* mess this up."

He nodded once, and we were both off. I zigzagged through the woods, parallel to the driveway until I saw Lilian's car. My blood boiled and then quickly chilled when I saw her and Craig Fisher talking.

My pulse felt as if it were out of control as I stood behind a tree, clear off the side of the driveway, careful not to crunch any branches, leaves, or debris, and tried to hear what they were saying. Nothing reached me. My instinct was to inch closer, but I remembered the stakes and peeked to see if I saw any cameras. Sure enough, there was a doorbell camera next to the front door, right near Craig's arm. What I wouldn't do to be a hacker instead of an artist. If I could get my hands on that recording...

I sighed and told myself that not getting caught came first. I peered out again and noted cameras looking out toward the woods but not in my direction. Craig Fisher wasn't as wealthy as the Carlsons, and I didn't think his security system was state-of-the-art. Probably it was something he would only look at if he got a motion alert. Better than my doorbell camera but not too sophisticated. But if I walked any closer or head-on, it could pick me up.

A door shut. I looked again. They were no longer out front. All I had to do was stick the coin-sized GPS tracker in a place where anyone would be unlikely to find it and leave. The best approach would be to crawl directly behind her car, using it for cover, which meant crawling on gravel.

It was painful and slow going, and my heartbeat thundered so loud I could barely hear the crunching gravel, but I could feel it painfully jabbing at my knees. A few minutes later, I was behind Lillian's car, and instead of using the wheel case like I had mentioned when I was thinking full throttle, I took my helmet off, got on my back, wiggled under the low car, and found the perfect place to stick the GPS tracker. I never heard the door open, but a low buzz of angry voices reached me just as I began to wiggle back out. When a tiny sharp rock stabbed a rib, I put my hand to my mouth. I jiggled, but the crunching gravel sounded like fireworks to my ears. I tried a shimmy instead, and it was more painful and slow going, but I managed to get out.

Or so I thought. When I moved to get on all fours and crawl, the remaining tassel on my shirt got caught under the tire. Craig's and Lillian's voices grew louder. They were angry and arguing, but all I could make out was Lillian saying, "You used me," and Craig yelling, "You used me first! Don't think I don't know. I figured it out soon enough!"

Possibly everything I could ever hope to know was being said. Tears of frustration welled in my eyes as my instincts warred with common sense. It took every fiber of my being not to stay and hear what they had to say. Finally, I pulled hard, but instead of releasing the tassel from under the tire, I tore it off. Either way, I was free.

I took advantage of the raised voices, crouched low, made my way to a giant Oak, and hid behind it. It felt like ages before I heard Lillian quickly reversing down the driveway. I waited a good few minutes before taking off the same way I came.

Anthony met me soon after, and we roared away. "You're a mess," he yelled over the engine. "Let's get you home."

"No. We'll be late to meet with Luke. And it's just dust from gravel. Let's stop at a gas station somewhere, and I'll get cleaned up. Just remind me never to use anything that dangles again," I yelled.

We stopped halfway to Fairborn, where Luke Wilson lived, and Anthony helped me clean myself up. I told Anthony what I'd overheard, and we just stared at each other. "You've connected Lillian to Sonrad's CEO."

I took in a deep breath. "Craig has always been good to me. He always listened to me and my theories...I—I can't trust him now. But we need more. It might simply be that he and Lillian are in a relationship now, and it's a coincidence." My heart was pounding. The thrill of progress was tempered by dread. I wasn't ready to examine my feelings on this.

"You carry monogrammed handkerchiefs?" I asked as I rubbed Anthony's handkerchief on my jeans in a gas station bathroom. "I haven't seen one since my Tío Roberto used one to wipe my nose after being attacked by a rooster at my bisabuela's house during her vigil."

"Keep still. You picked the wrong shirt to wear today." Anthony said as he used cheap toenail clippers we bought at the gas station's convenience store to cut off the loose threads that had once held tassels on my blouse. "*Tío?*" he asked when he was done.

"Uncle," I explained, grateful he was supporting my lame attempt to move away from the topic of Craig Fisher for the time being.

"*Bisabuela?*"

"Great grandmother."

"Why did a rooster attack you?"

"I didn't understand its mating rituals with the hens, and I tried to shoo him away. He was pecking at them. His name was Cesar, and he was mean and not very understanding. One of his wings got caught in my hair. It took seven people to calm and release him." Anthony laughed, and I smiled. My chest was still painfully constricted from having to leave without eavesdropping on Lillian's and Craig's argument, and smiling was welcome. "Monogrammed handkerchief?" I repeated.

"My *bisabuela* on my dad's side used to send them by the dozens when I was growing up. I set aside a few to remember her by but use the rest when I'm riding to tie around my face if I'm in traffic and exhaust fumes are bugging me."

I nodded and stuck it in my back pocket to clean and press for him when I got back home. *Bisabuelas* were rare, and gifts from them ought to be treasured. I then spread my arms out to ask if I looked decent.

He stepped back to assess me. "You'll do."

"Can we check the tracker now?"

"Sure thing." He brought out his burner phone. A tap on an app brought up a map. He zoomed in on a blue dot, and we saw Lillian was back at home. A few more clicks, and we saw she had gone straight home. Our eyes met, and we both grinned. It was working!

"Give me the phone," I said and stuck my hand out expectantly.

"I'm sorry, Angie, but I think I should keep it for your own good. You'll be tempted to look at it obsessively, and it won't do you any good. I promise I'll stay on top of it."

"But—" He pinned me with a stern look, and I knew he was right, though I wasn't sure I agreed being obsessive about this was a bad thing. I decided to try again later. Or sneak it away from him. "One thing that's been bothering me," I began instead, "is why Lillian has a burner car, so to speak, unless she's trying to hide something from Neil. But he must know about the Jeep because it's in his garage."

Anthony shrugged. "She normally drives a super recognizable car because she likes to stand out, but I think her husband would understand she needs a car for when she doesn't want to stand out, like maybe when she gets Botox or collagen injections for her lips, or when she sees a therapist, or at least tells him she's going to her therapist as an excuse."

I thought about this and realized he was right. "I see your point, though she doesn't get Botox. I'd be able to tell. Lip injections," I said, tapping my lips. "I'd say hyaluronic acid injections every six months."

"You could blackmail Hollywood actors with your observational skills," he said with a smile as he got back onto the motorcycle.

I got up behind him. "Too true. And yet here I am, a makeup artist for corpses."

Half an hour later, all smiles were gone. We were sitting in front of Luke, a wiry, distraught man of medium height and build, in the tiny living room of the duplex he had shared with Ronnie. "Chelsea mentioned that you two don't exactly get along," Anthony gently prodded. I was happy to leave the questions to him since he seemed to know where to go with them.

Luke looked up. "No, we don't," he said matter-of-factly. "It's my fault."

"How so?" I asked.

Luke sighed. "I found out from another friend that Chelsea thought I was using Ronnie to get close to Dan Martin for my career. I reacted badly and started in on Ronnie about him being only twenty-three and too young to get married and how she had dated Sheldon Douglas first and probably didn't know her mind." He shrugged. "Truth is, I probably did seek Ronnie out because of his dad early on. I wanted to be a sportswriter, and Dan Martin has his own column. But Ronnie became my best friend, and I'm big enough to admit that my motives weren't entirely pure early on. That changed, though, and I've never asked Ronnie or Dan Martin for anything."

Anthony and I exchanged a glance. That was a lot to pick through. "It's mature of you to admit that you were at fault," Anthony said, and Luke responded with another shrug.

"How long did Chelsea and Sheldon date?" I asked.

"A little over two years. Ronnie was a little conflicted about asking her out at first. He and Chelsea remained friends after she and Sheldon had broken up. One thing led to another, but Ronnie didn't want to break some unspoken code with his coach."

"So, there was no overlap between the two relationships?" Anthony clarified.

"No, not to my knowledge. And except for the last few months, Ronnie was an open book. He would've told me."

I nodded. "What was Ronnie's relationship with Sheldon like after that?"

Luke took a few moments to put his thoughts into words. "Ronnie trusted Sheldon as a coach, and he believed he had the team's best interest at heart, but he didn't trust him to have his *personal* best interest at heart. Sheldon was not a warm person. Dating Chelsea created more distance between Sheldon and Ronnie because Ronnie learned more about Sheldon's thought process regarding his players. He was very calculating and ambitious, leading Ronnie to keep him at arms' length off the field."

"How did Sheldon react when Ronnie said he was leaving?" I asked.

"Coldly, though he said all the right things. His teammates were all either happy for him or bummed about losing him. Not much ambiguity there."

After crossing something in his notes, Anthony glanced up, and I noticed he always did that when he was about to change the subject. "What did Ronnie call Sheldon?"

"Coach Sheldon," Luke answered with a shrug.

I shot Anthony a questioning look, and he nodded. We had agreed beforehand that we could mention *Shell* to Luke since Luke had no idea whom we had spoken to so far. He hadn't been the one to hire us, and we didn't owe him explanations. "Does the name Shell sound familiar to you?" I asked next.

Luke got a deer-caught-in-headlights look. After a long, awkward pause, he cleared his throat. "Why do you ask?"

My heartbeat picked up at his reaction. "We can't say. But clearly, it means something to you," I prompted.

Again, he hesitated. He brushed his fingers through his short, tight curls. His eyes darted from me to Anthony and then back again. "You're not detectives. I'm only talking to you because Mrs. Martin asked me to. Why is that?" he asked, his dark eyes meeting mine.

Anthony and I exchanged glances again. The more we used my ability to hear a person's last words to investigate suspicious deaths, the more questions we would need to learn how to handle. Right now, we didn't have time to discuss it. But I nodded at him to proceed as he saw fit because it was his grandfather's funeral home, and Mrs. Martin was their client. "I'm sure you heard about Mayor Sandberg's murder," Anthony began.

Luke shifted in his seat. "Yes, but I haven't kept up. I've been swamped."

"Well, Angie, my grandfather, and I solved her murder. I'm an experienced criminal defense lawyer, and my grandfather has been working in funeral homes since he was a little boy. Angie is a trained sculptor, and she recently started working with us on postmortem reconstruction. She notices the smallest details about people's features. It's hard to explain, but by working together and talking things through, Angie figured out some important details that others had missed. Anne Martin felt that we might help figure out what happened to Ronnie because she doesn't believe that he took his own life, and no one looked close enough. It's a long shot, we admit it ourselves, but..." Anthony glanced at me before proceeding. "Angie's parents were murdered twelve years ago, and it remains unsolved. My parents were killed by a drunk driver when I was only eight. We have a strong interest in figuring things out if we can because we empathize."

My stomach dropped so hard I felt the thud. Anthony's parents had been killed by drunk drivers when he was only eight years old? How in the world did I not know that? Yes, I'd only known him for a few days, but why hadn't it occurred to me to ask about his parents? He and Pappa were close. And Anthony's parents were never mentioned. It hadn't even occurred to me to ask about them. I already considered him and Pappa friends, and missing this detail shamed me.

In truth, I hadn't allowed myself to get too close to new people in twelve years. Therapists discussed my fear of abandonment stemming from my parents' murders with me, but I thought they were wrong because nothing could keep me away from my close-knit family, not even the fear of losing them. My parents had only taught me love. Realistic love. The kind where you could get angry, have your moments, and even grieve and experience fear, but still choose to give the best of you in the end. Until now, I had not realized that I kept new people at bay, never allowing myself to get too close.

"Fair enough." Luke's sudden, forceful words brought me back to the moment. There would be time enough later to sift through everything I was feeling. "But what I'm about to say can't be traced back to me." He met each of our eyes in turn.

"We promise we'll do our best," was Anthony's answer.

He blew out a breath. "I guess that'll have to do. This is bigger than me." He straightened. "Have you ever read the column, *Dear Tender Tim?*" Anthony and I both nodded. *Dear Tender Tim* was a popular advice column that had started in Wright State's newspaper and was now nationally syndicated. Tender Tim gave insightful advice, but he was unusually sensitive, which irked Abuela Nydia. She loved advice columns, even though she always disagreed with the advice. "Well," Luke continued. "I'm Tender Tim."

"You're Tender Tim?" I repeated, trying to reconcile the eloquent, thoughtful advice columnist with the nervous young

73

man in front of us. I tilted my head. Abuela Nydia felt Tender Tim tended to over-empathize. Maybe he over-felt in general?

He nodded. "It all started with a journalism professor and a project where I pretended to be writing an advice column, and it snowballed after that. Letters began pouring in, thanking me for understanding, and it hit me that my words can make a difference. I took it seriously after that, and it's something I take great pride in. But I would also like to remain anonymous. I don't know how seriously I'll be taken if it gets out that Tender Tim is only twenty-five years old. Ronnie was the only person who knew, aside from my journalism professor."

He got up and walked over to a backpack, took out a printed piece of paper, and handed it to us. "This letter came in two months ago. Look at the signature line," he instructed. I glanced down. *Empty Shell!* was the signature. Anthony and I looked at each other in shock. We shook our heads and began to read simultaneously, with Anthony holding the letter between us.

Dear Tender Tim,
My son and I recently donated blood together. Upon leaving, a nurse gave us our blood types, and my son got a funny look on his face when he saw mine. I decided to study blood types and was shocked to learn it was impossible that he was my son. Still disbelieving the evidence, I had a paternity test done. It confirmed my fears.
The truth is, I've never felt much of a connection with this young man. He doesn't look like his mom or me, and he and I have never had anything in common. I have always felt disappointed that none of my traits or inclinations were passed on to him. Now I know why. My very soul feels shattered by his mother's betrayal. There are NO WORDS. No words. Lately, I can't even look at him. I actively hate him with the same passion I still feel

for his mom. I can't and won't get over it. I'm sure he knows the truth. We are in opposite corners, circling each other, but I feel he is getting ready to approach me about it. I can't get over the betrayal, but I don't want to blow this wide open. How do I dodge? —Empty Shell!

Anthony and I looked at each other again for a long moment. No words indeed. Luke spoke first. "It's the most intense letter I've gotten yet, and I couldn't wrap my head around how awful and misguided this guy was. I showed it to Ronnie, so I could vent and get the poison out of my system before writing my advice. But Ronnie froze. He had already been acting strangely, but I chalked it up to the pressures of moving up a league and wedding planning. After the letter, though, he became numb to everything. All he cared about was soccer. He even started blowing Chelsea off. And I think you know where I'm going with this." He gave us a meaningful look. "I think his dad wrote it."

I took it all in before asking, "Why didn't you say anything when you found Ronnie?"

Luke sighed deeply. "Because I still have doubts. Because if I'm right, it gives Ronnie a motive for taking his life, which is the official cause of death anyway. And if Dan Martin didn't want to say anything, then who am I to potentially blow the Martins relationship up, especially now? It would make everything worse."

"Do you have any other evidence that this letter came from Dan Martin?" Anthony asked after a long, heavy silence.

Luke dropped his shoulders. "The soccer team held a blood drive around three months ago, and Dan and Ronnie donated together. Ronnie was happy his dad had agreed to go, but I think Mr. Martin did it more for show. They got along, but I've always felt that Mr. Martin *acts* like the proud father rather than *feels* like the proud father. Ronnie never said anything, but you could tell he felt it by how hard he tried to make Dan proud. It's all circumstantial, however. I have no way of knowing who wrote the letter."

"Can I take a picture of it?" Anthony asked.

Luke hesitated. "Do I have your word you won't reveal that I'm Tender Tim?"

Anthony looked him in the eye. "As long as it doesn't hinder any investigation that might arise from all this, you have our word. But if it becomes relevant, we'll have to share it with the police."

Luke considered it. "You're right. I understand."

"I enjoy your column," I added.

Luke smiled gratefully despite himself. "Thanks."

My gut feeling was that Luke was a good guy and had been an excellent friend to Ronnie.

We couldn't get anything of note from him after that, though he certainly had given us a lot to think about. I couldn't wait to be out of earshot from him. Before I could say anything, Anthony looked up from his phone and said, "The Jeep is still at the Carlson's."

I gave his arm a grateful look. The tracker was always at the forefront of my mind, but that's not what I had been thinking about. "Anthony, about your parents—"

Luke came out then and gave us an awkward wave. Anthony waved back before saying, "We'll talk about it some other time."

I studied him for a long moment and squeezed his hand. The right time would be up to him.

Both our phones dinged then, and I got mine out before Anthony could put the burner away and take out his personal one. "It's Pappa. He says Brenda's waiting for me." I looked up. "And he noticed something odd about Ronnie."

SIX

"Christmas Eve arrives for every pig…"

ABUELA LUCI'S PREFERRED LITERAL
TRANSLATION OF A SPANISH AND
LATIN AMERICAN SAYING WITH
MANY VARIATIONS. ABUELA NYDIA'S
PREFERRED, FIGURATIVE
TRANSLATION: *YOU CAN'T ESCAPE
YOUR DESTINY…*

Pappa met us at the front door, and before we could ask him what he had noted in Ronnie, he ushered me in the direction of his office. "Brenda Mumford mentioned how grateful she was to you after the memorial service, Angie, and I told her you wanted to ask her something that might help you with your parents' case. The moment felt right. She's waiting for you."

I gave the open door a light rap, and Brenda turned. "Hi Angie," she said with a tired smile. "Pappa said you have some questions for me."

Instead of sitting behind the desk, I sat next to her and asked her how she was holding up. It wasn't small talk. I truly wanted to know. I'd had a whirlwind few days, but Brenda had been through a tornado. The woman she had called mom for the last twelve years had turned out to be her deceased real mom's identical twin sister.

"As well as can be expected, I guess." She paused and appeared to consider her own words. "Probably better than expected. I think it takes a while for these things to hit you fully, but I've been thinking our minds were designed that way, so that distance can blunt the force of impact when they do."

I took that in. "I think you may be right."

"You've been a big help, Angie, and if there's anything I can do for you..." She shifted in her seat, neatly circling back to where we started.

"Yes," I hesitated. "I have a question about Tilly's and Lillian Carlson's relationship years ago." Brenda's expression soured, but I continued. "Lillian did Tilly's hair long after she stopped needing the job. I can't help but think there was a power dynamic at play there. Do you happen to know what it was or what their relationship was really like?"

Brenda picked some nonexistent lint off her designer black blazer's sleeve before clearing her throat and looking at me again. "You and I don't know each other well, Angie, but I'm grateful to you. I need to know why you're asking me this, however. The Carlsons are powerful and vindictive people. I don't have it in me right now to be in their crosshairs, but I'm also not afraid of them. If you explain why you want to know, I might share a few things."

I nodded, understanding. Neither of us knew the other one well enough. Instincts and gut feelings only went so far, but sometimes you had to leap. "I'm investigating my parents' murders, and I've learned that only one witness ever came forward. This witness said that my mom bragged that she'd be wearing an expensive necklace the night they were murdered. I know this isn't true, and I'm trying to figure out why this witness lied. I hope you can help me understand Lillian Carlson's past better because I'm almost certain she was this false witness." I took a deep breath and let it out. "I'm trusting you with a lot here, and it's not easy. Hopefully, it helps you trust me."

Brenda stared at the floor and was quiet for a long time until it made me feel uncomfortable and regretful. Finally, she looked up. "What I'm about to tell you happened years ago, and I've gotten over it, but that doesn't mean I like to dredge it up." I nodded. "Lillian had an affair with my dad right before she married Neil Carlson, and my mother called him out on it. I eavesdropped and heard almost the entire conversation." She paused and shook her head. "It was strange because my mom wasn't even upset. She had hired a private detective, and that's how she found out. But I think the private detective must have told her something else about Lillian because my mother seemed almost gleeful about what an idiot my dad had been. She called him a pawn, telling him that at least he wasn't as stupid as Neil, who was now the mark. She didn't explain anything more than that, though my father seemed baffled by her attitude and words. She liked to play games like that. To leave him wondering if she'd retaliate and what he'd been an idiot about. Later on, when I found out Lillian was regularly driving back to Cincinnati to do my mother's hair, I knew she was playing with Lillian too and had something on her." She looked at me steadily. "I don't know what it was. It may have been that her affair with my dad overlapped with her relationship with Neil and my mother had evidence, or it might have been more than that. I didn't want to know then, and I don't want to know now. My life since I married my husband has been one of purpose and peace until this past week. I'd like to go back to peace, which means I don't even want to think about those times and those people." Her words seemed to come from a deep place.

"I understand, and I'm grateful. I promise you I won't bother you again." We parted, and I went to find Anthony and Pappa. My pulse began racing, and I couldn't wait to dig into this and what Luke had said about Ronnie.

Minutes later, Pappa, Anthony, and I were in the preparation room. I realized I felt more at peace than I had in years. There was purpose here. We'd get Ronnie to look like the young man Anne and Chelsea had loved, and we'd try to get to the bottom of what happened to him.

"I got Pappa caught up on how we followed Lillian to Craig Fisher's. Did you learn anything new from Brenda Mumford?" Anthony asked.

"I did…but we have so much to do," I said, gesturing toward the morgue refrigerator against the wall where Ronnie now lay. "And I'm not sure where we should start." I looked at Pappa for direction.

"You weren't with Brenda for very long, so let's start with what you learned from her. There's a lot to discuss with Ronnie."

I gave him a grateful look and relayed everything Brenda had told me. "And at the gala, Ashleigh James told me that Tilly used to call Lillian *honeytrap*, and now Brenda says she heard her call

Neil a *mark*. Both had affairs with Lillian while they were married. She's beautiful, which could account for the honeytrap comment, and they were both powerful men, one in Cincinnati and one here in Dayton, which could make them a mark. Why did she target them, specifically? And did she have an affair with Craig Fisher, too? If so, why did she target *him*?" I put my nose in the air. "I hate this idea of a femme fatale. So cliché."

Anthony smirked. "I'd rather be the honeytrap than the mark. Jessup Sandberg, Neil Carlson, and Craig Fisher likely thought they were too smart and powerful to be taken in by anyone."

"While I would much rather be like my regular self, surrounded by none of that," Pappa inserted.

Anthony smiled and took out the burner phone tracking Lillian's Jeep. "No matter who is what, digging into Lillian's life seems to be the best use of our time. Sadly, the Jeep is still parked at their house." He put it away. I was still itching to take the phone away from him, much as I understood his reasoning for keeping it.

"What's our next step with her until she moves?" I asked as I ran through different options in my head. "Who else can we ask about her?"

Pappa put a hand on my shoulder. "Slow down. Nalissa was mugged right after leaving the Carlson's, and you were followed this morning. Whatever we do, we have to be more discreet in the future."

"Right." Anthony blew out a breath. "And until that Jeep moves, our best bet is to wait to hear what Nalissa has on her."

"Meanwhile, we have Ronnie's case." Pappa walked over to the fridge and slid Ronnie out. It was difficult, but I managed to drag my mind away from Lillian. They were right, and it helped to have something important to latch onto. "Remember how I said the cause of death was strangulation?" Pappa asked. He didn't look at us or wait for a reply. "I've seen many throughout the years: protruding eyes, swollen tongue, purple face, bright red spots inside his eyelids. As you can see, Ronnie has all of these. After embalming, it's much better, but Anthony saw him when we picked him up."

It was quite sad, and it made me determined to make him look like his old self for those who loved him. Pappa then pointed to Ronnie's neck. "His neck wounds also indicate strangulation due to hanging by suicide. It's raw in places from the struggle against the rope, and there are scratches on his neck that would usually indicate he tried to get free of it."

"But wouldn't that mean he wasn't committed to taking his life?" I asked.

Pappa shook his head. "I've talked about it with coroners and medical examiners throughout the years, and no matter how committed, there is always a struggle for survival. Human nature takes over. What I missed before was that his fingers would also be raw, especially with the number of scratches on his neck, from trying to get free." His voice grew agitated. "There would also be skin underneath his fingernails. It's doubtful the coroner cleaned the fingernails before he left the scene and before we cut him down, and I can't see how his fingers would have no marks on them when his neck is scratched up. I've thought it through, and I simply can't make sense of it."

We stared at Ronnie for a long time. Even to my untrained eye, the distinction between rope burns and fingernail scratches was clear. I went through everything Pappa said in my mind, and like him, I couldn't see how his fingers looked perfect.

Pappa waited for my eyes to clear before saying, "Let's go to the room I prepared upstairs, where we can track our suspicions."

We followed Pappa's slow progress up two sets of stairs to the third floor of the Funeral Home. It was my first time on this floor, and I took the opportunity to look around. There were three doors to the right and two on the left down a long hallway with floor-to-ceiling wood panels painted a soft white. The doors to the right all led to a large casket display room. I peeked into the wood-paneled room and saw about half a dozen caskets with different finishes and many beautiful urns. One of the doors to the left housed another office, which I guessed was Anthony's. The room beside it looked like a small version of the reception room, with only two armchairs and a loveseat. "For when a loved one or grieving family needs a moment to themselves, apart from other mourners," Pappa explained when he saw me looking. "And here," he said, stopping at the end of the hallway and signaling to the last wood panel to the left, "is our command center, as Anthony put it."

My eyes widened when he pushed against the panel, and it opened into a tiny room. Two large corkboards were leaning against opposite walls, and a small window looked out onto both the river and cemetery. Because of the way Riverside Funeral Home with angled, only Pappa's office and this room had that view. There was an old, heavy-looking, large oak desk under the window, with both printouts on my parents' case that I had given to Pappa this morning.

"As you can see," Pappa continued. "I've been too busy to set anything up, but I did get started on bullet points for both cases." He pointed to the corkboards, and each had index cards attached to them with different colored thumbtacks.

Anthony gave him a look. "I'll put the corkboards up."

"Don't get started," Pappa said, looking equally stern. "It's good for me to be climbing stairs and keeping active. I can hammer a nail to a wall just as well as you. Heck, I taught you."

I read over the bullet points in each corkboard while they argued, feeling increasingly buoyed by the succinct but thorough job Pappa had done. "You have a knack for this," I interrupted their argument.

Pappa beamed and sat at the desk. "Now tell me what you learned from Luke Wilson.

We took Pappa through our conversation with Luke. When we were through, he was holding his face in consternation. "A possible affair and deceit? By the very person who hired us?" He sighed. "What have we gotten ourselves into…" It was more of a statement than a question from a man who seemed more resigned than dismayed.

"The pursuit of justice and revenue, remember?" Anthony said with a grim smile.

"Let's run through everything we know first," I said, more for my benefit than theirs. We were juggling two cases, and my parents' case was fighting for precedence in my head, especially after reviewing the bullet points. But Ronnie's case was recent, and the first few days were critical if I had learned anything from Tito watching Dateline throughout the years. "We have evidence to support both a murder and a suicide. Figuring out why Ronnie would say *Remember Shell* before he died is crucial to figuring out the motive behind either. This isn't the same as Mayor Sandberg saying *Bonnie is dead*. The moment we learned of Bonnie, we knew the person and statement were related. This is more of a word game. Shell could refer to Chelsea or Sheldon, or even a shell as an object." I stopped. "But I think it's telling that Shell was capitalized in that letter Luke Wilson showed us, and it wasn't a regular signature line. It ended with an exclamation point. If Dan Martin wrote that letter—and judging from everything Luke told us, it's a possibility—then Ronnie was likely referencing the same Shell when he died. But what does it mean?" I paused, not sure where to go next.

"If we're on the right track here, Dan knows." Pappa looked at both of us in turn. "And our next logical step is to talk to him."

I began ticking off what we knew about Dan. "Luke said that he didn't seem like a proud or loving parent to Ronnie. He also didn't want the coroner to investigate, even though Anne requested it, and the alibi Anne gave for him was weak. Dan was also with Ronnie the afternoon before he died, and if he did write that letter, we know Dan *actively hated* Ronnie—strong words. So, what would the motive be? Did he just go nuts when his fears confirmed that Ronnie wasn't his? And why take it out on Ronnie? It was hardly his fault if Anne had an affair."

"But the letter also says he felt passion for her," Anthony pointed out. "Maybe Ronnie was going to tell his mom, and Dan didn't want it out in the open. He'd rather get rid of the evidence of the affair, so to speak, than confront it." He paused. "We need an excuse to talk to Dan that will hold up to scrutiny, and we have to figure out how we're going to get anything out of him. It won't be easy."

Pappa's eyes lit up. "Dan Martin won't like it, but Angie and I can show up to ask him his preferences about everything related to the service and funeral. Tonight will be perfect. Most people are at home on Sunday evenings, and Anne told me she'd be packing things up at the house Luke and Ronnie shared. We might catch Dan alone."

Anthony gave Pappa a skeptical look. "An unannounced house call by the undertaker? Really?"

"When he sees a harmless funeral director and his ditzy cosmetologist sidekick, he might let his guard down. We can say that we couldn't reach Anne to ask for his telephone number and that his wishes are important to us."

"Ditzy?" I repeated, crossing my arms over my chest.

Pappa grinned. "You'll pretend to be. It's easier to ask questions when you're non-threatening. I already look non-threatening because of my age and stoop."

Anthony released a resigned breath. "I guess it could work...." He glanced at me. "You won't believe the things he gets away with when he exaggerates his stoop. He parks the hearse without regard to parking lines and never gets a ticket. People even look on indulgently when he scrapes the entire toasted cheese off the top of new mac and cheese trays at all you can eat buffets. He says the indulgent smiles are patronizing, but he milks them every chance he gets."

I laughed, and it felt good. "OK then. How do we get Dan to talk?"

Anthony looked at his watch. "Let's all think on that and talk later. I have a bingo game to get to, and you and Pappa need to work on Ronnie. I'll be back before you leave for Dan and Anne Martin's house."

"Bingo?" I repeated, unable to tamp down my smile.

"Bingo night at area churches," Pappa said. "Best place to drum up business. Handing out branded pens only gets you so far."

"How about billboards?" I asked. I kept seeing cheesy billboards of Welcome Home Funeral Parlors, with their Brad Pitt look-alike director Mason Wiley holding his arms wide open, and his toothy smile was beginning to bug me. They'd handled my parents' funerals, and none of us had been happy about their pressure tactics while we'd been grieving. I saw their commercials on TV, too, but I didn't think Pappa could afford that right now.

Anthony gave me a sharp-eyed look and made a zipping motion with his hand and mouth, but it was too late. Pappa quickly began ranting about franchises, profits over people, and how the entire industry was losing sight of what mattered: people. I agreed with all of it, and soon we were both preaching. Anthony led us out of the office and down the hallway and stairs.

Anthony brought out the burner phone when we got to the reception room, and I stopped. It was like dangling a treat in front of Tito when he was driving me nuts by barking up at a squirrel when I was trying to walk him. I allowed myself to be distracted, vowing to bark up this tree again later.

The Cherokee was still at the Carlson's. Pappa was right. Most people spent Sunday afternoons and evenings at home with family.

Anthony left, and Pappa and I got started on Ronnie Martin.

I allowed myself to take a good look at Ronnie's face for the first time. I had been trying to remain impersonal because I knew I wouldn't be able to do this for long if I became too emotional. But it didn't feel respectful to work on him without grieving his lost life.

In college, I took a workshop on sketching personality into faces. Eyebrows upturned in the inner corners and facing downward in the outer ones, and wide, upturned lips indicated a friendly nature. An overpowering nose and strong jaw showed a determined one. The late Ronnie had the markings of a friendly and determined personality, but I'd never get to know him to find out for sure. Why this made me feel a sense of loss when there were plenty of people I'd never get to know, I didn't understand.

"Any man's death diminishes me because I am involved in mankind," Pappa said, and I glanced down and blinked because that's exactly how I felt. "John Donne, Meditation Seventeen," he explained. "I say it to myself before I begin to work on a person."

"I wish you had been the one to take care of my parents," I managed to say. My throat felt thick, and I held myself tensely to get a hold of the sudden emotion that had taken over me. "I'm sorry I didn't know about your son and daughter-in-law, Pappa. I found out today. You're my friend, and I should have known this about you," I continued. What else had I missed throughout the years because of not wanting to connect too deeply with others? My parents would not have wanted that.

I sensed him observing me. After a moment, he covered my hand with his. "We *are* friends, Angie, because of the invisible bonds that were instantly formed. It all happened for a reason. I'm sure of that. The three of us have faced unimaginable loss and tragedy, and we will continue to grieve it together, even as we live, even as we thrive."

We remained like that for a long time, a feeling of peace passing from Pappa to me and, I hoped, back to him as I calmed down.

Soon, we were working on Ronnie with the same companionable peace we experienced while working on Mayor Sandberg. The reconstruction process was different from the process for Mayor Sandberg, and Pappa explained the main differences between working with someone young and an older person.

He had me coat eye caps with petroleum jelly to help keep the shape of Ronnie's eyes and prevent them from dehydrating and inject bleach to help with extravascular discoloration. I glanced at the photo we were working with, and it amazed me how he began to look like himself again little by little. After two hours, a combination of trained eyes, known techniques, and creative thinking had Ronnie looking like the friendly young man in the photo.

Now, more than ever, I wanted to solve this case. "After asking him the usual questions about preferences, I think we should ask Dan Martin if the name Shell means anything to him," I suggested to Pappa.

Pappa took a deep breath and let it out. "I was thinking along the same lines. It will give us the reaction we need, but we must be careful. We don't know if Dan's a murderer. *I* will be the one to ask him, Angie, and only if he is clearly without weapons or any means of immediately hurting us. I'll bring my Glock and give you my taser."

I nodded. "I have pepper spray, too."

"Good. But we should leave before Anthony gets back," Pappa suggested. I grinned, delighted that he was willing to leave without Anthony because I had been thinking the same thing. Pappa and I together did not look threatening at all. A house visit might look odd, but our excuses could be believed. Anthony, with his muscles and always sharp gaze, would raise suspicion. "And let's take the hearse," he continued. "It will give anyone at home a clear indication of who we are."

"Do you mind stopping by the house first?" I asked. "Because I need to give my dog Tito some love and let him out." I wondered if I would have to start bringing Tito over to Abuela's on

Sundays so he wouldn't be lonely if I were going to be out attempting to solve murders.

We went down a back alley in case neighbors were still waiting to pounce on me about Mayor Sandberg, and Pappa walked up with me to meet Tito, who was barking up a storm. "He did what? How rude!" I replied.

"What's he saying?" Pappa asked, amused.

"His nemesis, a furry Shih-Poo from down the street, keeps peeing in our yard. And he does it on purpose." At least he wasn't protesting that I'd left him behind on a Sunday. By the looks of it, he'd been entertaining himself with the peanut butter-filled toy I had left him.

We walked Tito down the street, so he could poop, pee twice, and clean his paws roughly enough to throw debris toward the Shih-Poo's house. I bagged his business and brought a trotting Tito and his proud, upright tail home. Soon, we were off, leaving a contented Tito curled up on my reading chair, with the TV turned on to a Telenovela on Univision.

Dan and Anne Martin's home was a twenty-minute drive away in Centerville, in a meticulously planned and manicured neighborhood of McMansions, each set on half to one-acre wooded lots. "Not one weed anywhere," Pappa observed.

"How can you tell? Some weeds look like flowers and plants to me, but one of my neighbors, Mrs. Shoehorn, assures me they're weeds when they pop up in my yard."

Pappa grinned. "One person's weed is another person's flower."

We drove up the long driveway of the Martins' Colonial revival and parked close to the walkway.

The house's interior was dark, except for a faint light illuminating the side yard to our right. Somber, classical music reached us from the same direction. Pappa leaned in and whispered. "Chopin's Funeral March."

Maybe Dan Martin *was* mourning, then, and Luke was wrong about him. Instead of giving voice to the thought, I shifted my head and eyes to the left to show Pappa that there was a doorbell camera right in front of us.

We rang it first and knocked after a minute or two, but nobody came to the door. "Maybe Mr. Martin went with his wife to Luke and Ronnie's house in Fairborn," I suggested, ensuring the doorbell camera caught my words. "That's too bad," Pappa replied in a similar tone. "It would be nice to get the rest of the family's feedback for the viewing." Another two minutes passed, no one came to the door, and we went back to the hearse.

"I think someone may be at home, and we're understandably being ignored. After all, they are grieving, and we're two strangers on their doorstep," Pappa said with a shrug.

"Can I drive?" I asked. Pappa threw me the keys. I hit reverse and stopped at the end of the driveway, where the doorbell camera could no longer see us.

Pappa sighed. "What are you doing?"

"Can you see any other security cameras around?" I asked, searching the perimeter once more. "I want to take a quick peek into that room with the lights on."

He searched, too. "I don't see any, but what possible excuse do we have to go looking through windows, Angie? It's unconscionable to be so intrusive with a grieving family."

"Under normal circumstances, I would completely agree and be appalled by my suggestion," I said as I climbed out. "But these aren't normal circumstances. I want to see if he looks like he's grieving. If he does, it could mean that Luke was wrong about him."

"A murderer can still grieve."

I considered that. "True. But if he's waltzing around the room to Chopin's Funeral March, then it's a clue that he's not grieving."

"You want a murderer catching you looking through his window?"

"It's dark, and it's the side of the house facing the woods. If I go wide, I can come up behind a tree, look in without being seen, and come back."

"Fine," Pappa huffed. He got out and came around to the driver's side. "I see this may have to be a getaway car again."

I ran out, went wide, came up behind a maple tree, took my quick peek, and turned to ice. No window. Just an open sliding door. And a dead body.

SEVEN

"To great evils, great remedies."

ABUELA LUCI'S PREFERRED LITERAL
TRANSLATION FOR A POPULAR
SPANISH AND LATIN AMERICAN
PROVERB. ABUELA NYDIA'S
PREFERRED FIGURATIVE
TRANSLATION: *DESPERATE TIMES
CALL FOR DESPERATE MEASURES.*

I stood there, hand to stomach, mouth agape, staring at the body. Stocky, muscular, with a mass of dark hair, like in the pictures Anne had brought. It looked like Dan Martin, sitting in his office chair, head on his desk, knife in his back, blood all over his pink polo. "Pappa!" I finally choked out.

Moments later, Pappa was beside me, panting. "Angie!" he gasped when he looked past the sliding door. I took off on a sprint toward Mr. Martin without thinking, but Pappa held me back. "Don't! You could destroy evidence, such as footprints." He glanced at the ground. "We may have destroyed some already, and the murderer could still be around! We need to call 911." He pulled me toward the car and whipped out his phone while looking around.

"Wait! What if he's still alive? We should try to save him!"

"I'll check," he called over his shoulder as he shifted gears and hustled toward the house. "If he's still alive, I'll try to stem the blood flow, but the murderer could still be inside. Get in the car and call 911."

"No—if he's dead, I need to hear his last words!"

"You're right." Pappa cursed and quickened his pace. "I'll call 911 while I check if he's alive. You go to the car, get my Glock and gloves, and meet me inside." Pappa hurried through the sliding doors before I could argue against him going in alone. It was hard to think straight, but I sprung into motion.

I ran to get the Glock, an entire box of nitrile gloves, and joined Pappa, all the while looking down to make sure I didn't destroy footprints. My heart began pounding so hard when I saw the body up close that I could barely hear Pappa speaking to the operator.

"Dead," Pappa announced the moment he hung up. "But his body is still warm. The operator said to lock ourselves inside and not touch anything." He pulled a pair of gloves on and took the gun from me to set it on the desk so I could do the same. He then carefully closed and locked the sliding door.

Chills ran down my spine. "Do you think the murderer is still in the house?

"They might have escaped through the sliding door, and that's why it was open." He looked around again. "The door to the study is locked, but it's also possible the murderer locked it before shutting it if they left that way instead."

"And they might have a key." Careful not to smudge any possible fingerprints, I jammed the doorknob with a nearby chair, came back, took a deep breath, and tried to slant over Dan's head without disturbing him. It was too difficult to manage without stumbling. "You'll have to hold on to my shirt in the back," I instructed Pappa. Pappa grabbed my shirt, and I leaned in. At least there were no nearby neighbors who could see us through the sliding door. Although the murderer could still be out there, in the woods, watching us. I shook off the thought and focused on listening carefully. "*We can go away together. I won't turn you in—agh! Uh.*" Whispered words ended with a cry of pain, a final sound, and a final breath.

"I can't hold you much longer," Pappa groaned, pulling me back. "Did you hear anything?" he gasped. I nodded, but he put a hand up before I could tell him what I heard. "Tell me later. Let's get our story straight. We're witnesses now, Angie, and sticking to the truth is best."

"Which truth?" I asked, wondering if he wanted to out me and my ability. I could feel a headache coming on just thinking about it.

"The truth about why we came here and decided to look through the sliding door." He put his arms on my shoulders and took me through it. "We'll explain that Anne wanted us to look closer at what happened to Ronnie because of our success with Mayor Sandberg. We heard the music and wondered if he was grieving and decided to peek from afar. When we saw the body, knife, and blood, we thought he might still be alive, and that's why I came inside to check and call 911 while you got a gun and gloves to keep us and the scene safe. The body was still warm, and we barricaded ourselves in the room if the murderer was still around but were careful not to touch anything. Now let's look around to see if we find any clues. And let's take pictures! Just remember: *don't disturb anything!*" Sirens sounded faintly in the distance.

We didn't have much time, but I wanted to be smart about our search. I took a good, quick look around. It was a beautiful study, full of quarter-sewn oak trim and built-ins, heavy, white oak furniture, seascapes, and embossed ivory wallpaper. A sweet scent filled the air. A gun on the floor beside Dan Martin looked like it could have fallen from his hand. Some pretty yellow and white flowers were lying on the desk. A noose was hanging from the tall ceilings. Had someone tried to stage another suicide, and had it all gone wrong? I took pictures of it all.

The bottom desk drawer was open. A glance told us it held files. "See how there's a divide between those two folders? Someone was looking for something there. We may even have interrupted them. Let's see what they were looking at," I exclaimed as I squatted down. The sound of different sirens grew closer. A fire truck was on its way, too. I quickly but carefully checked. "Pappa! It's a trust agreement for Michelle "Shell" Young!" Pappa and I stared at each other for a long moment, hardly believing what we'd found.

The fire truck honked. Sirens drew near. We shook ourselves out of our trance, I took a picture of the trust agreement, and we both shuffled off to a corner, looking appropriately shocked and shaken. It wasn't an act. I looked around the room again, but nothing else seemed out of place. My mouth was dry, and my head was beginning to throb. Pappa had a hand to his head, and he was sweating. "Centerville is the Montgomery County

Sheriff's jurisdiction," he said. "They know me, and no matter how we explain it, they'll be surprised I intruded on a grieving family by peeping through windows."

I put my hand on him to reassure him. "They also know me, and nobody there will be surprised I decided to take a quick look. As you said, we'll stick to the truth. You didn't leave the hearse until I saw the body and called to you." But then it hit me: Centerville was *Montgomery County jurisdiction.* No matter how much questioning I was put through tonight, Lieutenant Brian Mahoney would be sure to follow up with more the moment he found out I was involved. *Ugh!* Hopefully, I could stop him from getting anywhere near me again with the magic cousin Wanda explained. The moment I got home, I'd find that box of colored candles and perform an intense candle meditation in the light of the now waning moon.

Red and blue lighted the room, and we waited until we saw a fireman outside the window before moving to open it. "I'm glad to get out of here," Pappa said.

I looked at Dan Martin and all the blood I had worked to ignore and shivered. "Me, too."

We were questioned separately, and I stuck to our truth. It did not go over well. Sergeant Beemer forcefully pointed out that I had outed Tessa Baker as the mayor's murderer by almost getting shot by her. I decided it was not the time to say I had figured it out a few seconds before. With a silent apology to Tender Tim, I also revealed the information Luke Wilson had told us about the letter, the blood donation, and the way Ronnie had reacted to the letter.

The coroner asked to speak privately with Sergeant Beemer, and she left me. Soon the body was transferred to a van. I was eager to talk to Pappa, but we knew better than to confer about anything until we were alone and not being watched.

When Sergeant Beemer came back, she had rapid-fire questions for us both. They centered on what we heard and saw when we got there—and circled back to what we were doing there in the first place.

Anne arrived, frenzied and with a terrified look in her eye as she demanded to know what was going on. Sergeant Beemer gave us a stern look. "Don't leave until I give you the signal. We might have additional questions." She left to talk to Anne.

The moment I found out my parents had been murdered came back to me, and I couldn't look at Anne as she was informed about her husband's death. Pappa tactfully turned away, too.

In the end, Anne confirmed that she had asked us to investigate Ronnie's murder. We were finally told we could go, but a hysterical outburst from Anne stopped us in our tracks. "*That woman* was Dan's first wife, and she cheated on him with his best friend. *His best friend!* He and I had been married for three years when she got cancer and manipulated him into leaving me to be there for her. And then Shell got pregnant by Dan and died giving birth to Ronnie. But *I* became Ronnie's mother!" she sobbed.

I looked down but remained riveted. Abuela would say it was like the plot to *Mi Querido Abandonado,* the biggest tear-jerker we'd ever watched. But it wasn't. It was all so real; it made everyone uncomfortable. I wished they would all sit with their discomfort and feel as deeply as possible. Maybe then they'd genuinely listen to those of us left behind. Even my wise and beloved abuelas had trouble witnessing grief.

The detective asked something, and Anne, weeping softly, said, "I forgave him eventually, but only because Shell gave me Ronnie. Do you hear me? *Shell* gave me Ronnie. She said she knew I'd be a better parent than her or Dan. I forgave him because I wanted Ronnie to have both a mother and father." She took a deep, shaky breath and calmed down some, but her voice still carried. "I didn't know that she had lied to him and cheated on him again in the end. I didn't know Dan wasn't Ronnie's father, but I don't care, and I'm not surprised. *I* raised Ronnie. *I* loved Ronnie. *I* took him to every soccer practice. Why would I care that Ronnie wasn't his biological son?" She wiped at her eyes and nose. "He was the sweetest child." She looked at the detective. "All I ever asked from Dan in return for my forgiveness was not to tell Ronnie who his biological mom was. I couldn't have him know it wasn't me, not when Ronnie would hug me with those chubby little arms and look at me like I was magic. Ronnie was the only person who ever truly loved me." Her voice broke. "And without Shell and Dan, I'd never have had Ronnie..."

———

It was almost ten when we were finally on our way back to the funeral home. Pappa was still looking dazed, but he insisted on driving. I felt as if I had just woken up from a strange nightmare, with my mind foggy and my head aching. "I can't stop thinking about Anne," I said. Her pain had been difficult to behold. Not only had she lost a son and her husband, but she had relived his betrayal. "And I wonder why she didn't tell us she wasn't Ronnie's biological mom if she wanted us to look at every angle." I shook my head. "I can't even begin to understand what it could all mean."

Pappa sighed deeply, and when he spoke, his voice was thick. "She loved Ronnie deeply. That much was clear. He was her son, and maybe she wanted to avoid labels like *biological* or *adoptive*. She never even told Ronnie, even though she must've known deep inside that he should know." We were quiet for a while until Pappa said, "The sheriff's office will take over now, and they'll hopefully unravel everything, but now that we know Dan's last words, we need to keep an eye on things. How about you search your phone so we can learn a little bit more about Shell Young?"

"Anthony has texted and called at least half a dozen times," I said when I took out my phone.

"I know," Pappa said with a tired sigh. "We'll deal with him soon enough."

Search results showed that Michelle "Shell" Young was an artist and socialite from Cape Cod, Massachusetts, known mainly for her seaside paintings and because her family was old money. She had died of breast cancer twenty-four years ago. All searches brought up mostly resales of her artworks. She was well known locally but didn't have enough clout nationally for me to find anything else on her.

Soon we were back at the funeral home, both of us thirsty enough to drink several glasses of water but too nauseous about everything that had happened to eat. We found Anthony in our new "command center," putting up the second corkboard on the wall to the right of the window. The first one, with notes on my parents' case in Pappa's handwriting, was already set up on the opposite wall. Index cards strewn on the oak desk showed Anthony had been working on notes about Ronnie's case.

Before we could tell him anything about the evening's shocking turn of events, we had to endure a furious round of questions about where we had been and why we hadn't waited for him or informed him of where we were going. "I should put trackers on both of you." He folded his arms and glared down at us as if we were wayward children.

"Dan Martin is dead, and Ronnie Martin wasn't Anne's biological child either," Pappa blurted the moment he was able to get a word in. "The late *Shell* Young, Dan's first wife, was Ronnie's biological mother. She left him a trust. We have a picture of the document."

That got Anthony to drop his arms and stop his rant.

I continued. "And Dan's last words were, '*We can go away together. I won't turn you in.*' We also have pictures of the crime scene. There was a gun on the floor and a noose hanging from the ceiling."

After further filling a mesmerized Anthony in on the particulars, we pulled up the photos of the crime scene and the trust agreement. It was for one million, three hundred and seventy-five thousand dollars and set up for Ronald Martin to be distributed in a lump sum on his twenty-fifth birthday.

A clause also addressed what would happen if Ronnie didn't make it to his twenty-fifth birthday. "If Ronnie died, it would all go to Anne Martin," Pappa read.

"How old was Ronnie?" I asked.

"His twenty-fifth birthday would've been in January…" Pappa's voice trailed off, and a moment later, he shook his head. "But I know grief, and Anne's was palpable. She was also genuinely distraught tonight when she talked about her love for Ronnie. I have a hard time believing she'd hurt him in any way."

We looked to Anthony, hoping he'd share some insight, but he continued to stare at the floor as if the answers were written on the cold white tiles.

Pappa shrugged and turned to me. "I've been thinking that Dan's last words suggest that he was negotiating for his life, telling whoever wanted him dead that he wouldn't turn them in and that he would go away with them." He put his hand to his head, and I knew he felt the same way I did. It had been a long few days, and even thinking was starting to hurt.

I took a deep breath. "Let's start at the beginning. Anne Martin and Chelsea both believed that Ronnie was murdered, but the scene was set up to make it look like suicide. Ronnie's last words imply that his death had to do with Shell Young. Dan's crime scene photos could suggest that someone was trying to stage a suicide by hanging with him, as well, but Dan pulled a gun, and it all went wrong." Was that too speculative? I wasn't sure. "So far, Anne is the only person with a motive for killing Ronnie, but she's the one who kept pushing for an investigation. And why would she want Dan dead, too?"

Anthony strolled around the embalming table. "What I find curious is that Anne didn't tell us about the trust agreement when we asked her for motives. It makes no sense that she would want us to dig but not tell us that."

Pappa looked up. "It's possible she didn't know about it."

Anthony stopped walking and looked back. "But she also didn't tell us she wasn't Ronnie's biological mom. And she came to us, amateurs, instead of hiring a private detective or insisting that the police investigate. Maybe Chelsea was the one who was insisting, and Anne came to us to appease her."

Pappa picked up one of the index cards on the desk and turned it around his fingers. "I think Anne came to us because she never adopted Ronnie; therefore, she wasn't the next of kin. She had limited rights. Dan was the one insisting they accept the suicide and move on."

Anthony shrugged. "I guess the trust could also be a motive for Dan to kill Ronnie. He was married to Anne and would benefit from the windfall, and he didn't love Ronnie anyway. Learning that Ronnie wasn't his son and knowing that his twenty-fifth birthday was coming up could have been the catalyst. But then Anne wouldn't stop pushing for an investigation, and Dan got spooked." He stopped and shook his head. "But then why would he say *I won't turn you in?*"

"It does make it sound like he was talking to the killer." It was my turn to put my hand to my head.

Pappa plopped himself down in a chair. "Look, I'm as eager to solve this as you are, but we're forgetting that we are likely off the case now. Dan Martin was transferred to the Montgomery County morgue. Montgomery County Sheriff's Office will take over now, and Anne Martin has two tragedies on her hands."

Anthony gave a reluctant nod. "The only thing we had on our list for tomorrow was to talk to the soccer team, and I still think we should because we know both Ronnie's and Dan's last words, and talking to them can give us some more insight. But Pappa's right. We should leave it to the sheriff's department and only intervene if they get stuck."

I gave him a skeptical look. "How would we intervene?"

Anthony ran a hand through his hair. "I have no idea. As Pappa says, all we can do is take it one step at a time. For now, we have more time to spend on your parents' case. Let's hope Nalissa doesn't dodge us again tomorrow."

"I won't let her! I swear I'll hunt her down! Maybe we should put a tracker on her, too."

Pappa rolled his eyes. "No more talk of trackers from either of you."

"Okay. But while we're still on the subject…" I looked at Anthony expectantly.

Anthony smiled for the first time since we'd gotten back. He pulled the burner phone out of his back pocket and glanced down. "The Jeep is still in the Carlsons' garage. I've checked a few times, and it hasn't moved again today."

"Well," Pappa said with finality. "There's nothing left for us to do today. It's been a long couple of days, and I say we all try to get some rest so we can match wits with Nalissa tomorrow."

I nodded. "I also have to match wits with Abuela. She's coming over tomorrow for a Zoom meeting with my cousin Wanda, and I have no idea what they're up to."

Anthony drove me home and walked me to the door, still scolding me about going to the Martins without him until Tito advanced on him, growling long and low. Only my Abuelas were allowed to berate me in Tito's presence. A neighbor had once tried, and Tito had bared his teeth at him while growling so low and hard, his suddenly tick-straight tail and tucked-back ears had vibrated with anger.

Anthony backed away, and I gave him a half-smile and half-wave. We hadn't consulted with him, we'd left him behind, and he felt we had put ourselves in danger. I couldn't blame him for trying to make sure we didn't do it again, but I didn't regret our actions either.

Tito seemed agitated and kept trying to get me to the back door, but he wasn't twirling around like he did when he needed to go. I figured he had been hounded by nosy neighbors out front all day, and he wanted to make sure I took him to the backyard to do his last business of the day instead of taking him to the front.

I went upstairs to my bedroom closet to look for the candles Wanda had given me when I was five. Though my head was still pounding, and my stomach felt queasy, the thought that Lieutenant Mahoney would soon find out I had been at the scene of a possible murder tonight kept me going. My motivation to get rid of him was stronger now than in the morning.

Tito followed with his tail tucked up between his legs. I told him about my day, asking him to please take it easy on Anthony the next time he saw him. Tito tilted his head to the side when he saw the candles, and I told him we were about to do some magic out back. He understood the *out back* part because he ran back downstairs, and I could hear him scratching at the back door. "Be right there," I called, grabbing a wide-bottom aluminum pot my Abuela Nydia had sent over from Puerto Rico (insisting no other one would do for medium-grain white rice), a candle holder, a skewer, a lighter, and a dog biscuit.

When we went outside, Tito began to sniff around like a hound dog. I called him over with the dog biscuit, and he came over to chew on it beside me, watching me now with interest. I used the skewer to carve Brian Mahoney's name on the candle, from the bottom to the top, as Wanda instructed. I then placed the candle in the candle holder, put it in the middle of the aluminum pot, picked up the lighter, and focused hard on visualizing Brian Mahoney walking away from my life. I held the vision in my mind, working hard to feel its power, and loudly chanted, "*Of Brian Mahoney set me free…*" but then hesitated on this next part, half-afraid that the universe would not agree.

I shook my head, straightened, and decided my will would have to be stronger than the universe's will. *I picked up Tito and held him close on a whim* because it made me feel more connected to life.

I lit the flame and chanted, "*Of Brian Mahoney, set me free,*" loud and clear. "*If the universe so agrees!*"

A sound like thunder exploded through the night. For a moment, the world was all smoke and debris, suspended in time, the only sound my ringing ears and pounding heart.

EIGHT

"Where there was a fire, ashes remain."

SPANISH AND LATIN AMERICAN
SAYING

I was thrown back and fell hard. Tito was still tucked into my arms. Patio furniture lifted off the ground around me. Instinct kicked in. I crawled away, hugging Tito, while projectiles rained down on my back.

Ears still ringing and vision hazy, I hauled myself up and tried to see through the smoke, but I wasn't sure which way to go. I ended up in the street, with people shouting and sirens blaring. I stumbled onto the pavement and was soon surrounded by neighbors, but I couldn't hear what anyone was saying. My only reaction was to swat hands away and not let anyone take Tito away from me. He was tenderly licking my arms, and he would not be happy to be separated from me.

"The candle. The flame. The universe…" I tried to explain to the faces hovering over me, but I knew no one would understand. I looked toward my house. Fire engulfed the kitchen.

Concerned faces peered into mine. I closed my eyes, tried to think, and the scene began to make some sort of sense. An explosion. In my kitchen. "Is everyone here okay?" I croaked, opening my eyes again. Thinking about my nosy but wonderful neighbors and their pets had me blinking back tears. Had they been hurt? I was assured everyone was okay.

A fire truck soon arrived. Thank goodness I lived only a few blocks away from the fire station. Someone picked me up, and I looked up to see a firefighter's face shield. Again, they tried to take Tito away from me, but I wouldn't let them. "It was the universe. It's trying to tell me something, but I don't know if it agrees or disagrees with my request," I explained as she sat me down on a stretcher. "Shh," she hushed me. I wanted to try to explain again, but the sight of paramedics and open ambulance doors stopped me. An image of Abuela Nydia getting a Google alert about an explosion at my house had me sitting up. My Abuelas would handcuff me to their sides for life if this landed me in the hospital. "I'm fine! I'm fine!" I tried to climb down, but they wouldn't let me.

I took a few calming breaths and sorted through my thoughts. No one would believe I was fine unless I acted like I was okay. I tried a quick self-assessment. "I'm a little sore from where debris hit my back and legs, and the skin there stings, but I feel fine. I was lifted away from the blast. I protected Tito, and he's been alert and conscious the entire time, as have I. But you can check our vitals," I offered. Although I had held Tito to me, and his heart rate felt normal, I wanted to make sure his little body was okay.

Our vitals were checked, and everything was within normal range. I refused to be taken to the hospital. After they treated my wounds, they asked if they could call anyone for me, and I hesitated. It was a miracle Albert Witherspoon hadn't broken down Abuela's Luci's door to tell her the latest. If he had, Abuela would be here. Unless she was in the backwoods of some state visiting another cousin I'd never heard of. I looked at the time. It was almost eleven. Reluctantly, I gave them Anthony's number. A man in plainclothes approached me then, and I saw there were two news vans parked nearby. Shoot. Google alerts once again swam before my eyes.

The paramedic was about to shoo him away, but I stopped her. "I'm up to answering a few questions." The first one was my name, which I had been banking on. "Annie Perez," I lied. The paramedic hid a smile but didn't contradict me. Hopefully, it would create enough confusion to buy me time before Abuela Nydia heard about it. I said no one was hurt and tried to make the whole thing sound as exciting as a firecracker going off on a sidewalk.

The reporter moved to leave, and Lieutenant Brian Mahoney, dressed in jeans and a black t-shirt, came into view. He was conferring with firefighters and police, and one of the paramedics walked over to him. Likely to say that my vitals were good and that I was refusing hospital care. I leaned forward and was able to pick up bits and pieces of the conversation. Only secondary blast injuries, no primary or tertiary blast injuries likely. A firefighter said something about the kitchen, powder room, and living room. The blast hadn't been enough to bring down the house, but it would be shut up until it could be inspected. At least, that's what I understood from a distance. Mahoney turned to me, and our eyes met. He looked like he had aged ten years. There were lines on his face, and his jaw was tense. A firefighter walked over to him, holding the candle.

"No," I shouted and propelled myself off the stretcher, running toward them, but it was too late.

"Your name is written on this candle we found out back," the fireman said to him. He then glanced over at me, looking a little fearful, as if I were crazy.

"Give that to me, please," I said, stretching my hand out when I halted to a stop before them.

"It's evidence," another older firefighter said gruffly.

I closed my eyes. Evidence. There was a candle with a law officer's name on it, and there had been an explosion. Even if there was no apparent connection between the two, it certainly didn't look normal. Explaining now would be better than being hauled off somewhere for an interrogation. I opened my eyes. Five people were staring at me, waiting. I looked down at my arms, where I was still holding Tito, and noticed that all the tiny hairs were singed.

"Who absolutely *has* to be here for my explanation?" I asked

Brian Mahoney, the gruff firefighter, and a police sergeant raised their hands. I looked pointedly at the paramedic, another firefighter, and another policeman. Their superiors signaled for them to leave.

"Do I still have eyebrows?" I asked because I caught the police sergeant looking at me in a funny way.

Brian ran a hand through his hair, "You look fine, Angie, except that your shirt is in tatters, which, may I remind you, started this morning when you left one of your tassels hanging on my fence."

His eyes were blazing, and I was surprised he had allowed himself that little outburst. The firefighter and police sergeant looked between the two of us with increasing interest. "And if we're looking at you funny, maybe it's because you've almost been killed two nights in a row." He pointed the candle at me. "Explain."

I swallowed hard. "Well, my grandmother is Señora Lucinda, the owner of Tea and Spirits, so I'm sure it will be no surprise that I believe in magic…" The most humiliating ten minutes of my life followed as I explained how Lieutenant Brian Mahoney kept showing up in my soup, so to speak, and how I had asked my cousin Wanda, a renowned witch from Brooklyn, for a spell to draw him away from me. This was met with understandable skepticism, and I had to call Cousin Wanda so she could back up my story. Cousin Wanda loved an audience, and she was delighted to explain it all to them, even though she was wearing a green clay mask and a shower cap.

"See you tomorrow, Angie," she said with a wink. "I'm glad you weren't hurt."

The gruff firefighter was no longer looking so gruff. I noted pursed lips and averted eyes as if he were trying not to laugh or smile.

Indeed, it was no laughing matter. Part of my house had exploded, and someone could have been killed.

The sergeant looked confused. "I'm still trying to understand what you meant about Lieutenant Mahoney being in your soup."

They began to pepper me with questions again. At first, they centered around everything I had done the past few days as if they were trying to determine if I had somehow caused the explosion.

"Have you noticed any strange smells that could signal a gas leak?" the gruff firefighter asked.

"No. Not at all."

"Any zapping, hissing, buzzing, or snapping noises that could signal a short circuit?"

On they went, and all I could answer was "no."

"Do you know of anyone who would want to harm you?" the sergeant asked.

I avoided Brian Mahoney's intense gaze. "N—no." There was no way I would reveal I had made headway into my parents' case, not when I couldn't trust anyone to stay out of it and let me see it through. "Unless someone's angry that I figured out Tessa Baker was Mayor Sandberg's murderer or that I'm asking questions about my own parents' case. But I've been doing that for years." There. The truth with only necessary omissions. "People have been loitering around my house the last few days, mostly because they were curious about Mayor Sandberg's case," I continued. "And it grew worse today because of the whole thing with Tessa Baker last night. But mostly, it was neighbors. I can't be sure if strangers were around, too, because I've been escaping through the back alley, but I don't think anyone would have gotten past my neighbors."

The fact that Mahoney didn't speak up when he knew some of what I had been up to the past few days and that I had possibly been followed this morning was suspicious. It reinforced that he had his own agenda. We eyed each other a moment, distrust palpable in both directions.

It occurred to me then that Tito had been acting strangely when I got home, wanting to check out the back porch and then sniffing one corner of it, and I relayed this to them, excited because it felt like a clue. This seemed to interest them. "What evidence have you found so far?" I asked and received a standard non-answer.

"Can I talk to her alone for a moment?" Mahoney asked when the questions wound down. The moment they were out of earshot, he turned to me. "The best way to get rid of me, Angie, is to stop getting yourself into dangerous situations."

"It's my fault that my house exploded?" I asked hotly. I deserved a little bit of sympathy, didn't I? I could've been inside! Tito barked, and I petted him until he settled down again.

"When the police sergeant asked if anyone would want to harm you or if you've noticed any suspicious activity, you left out that a car was following you this morning."

"If you thought it was important, why didn't you say anything to the sergeant?"

He ignored me and continued, "A car was following you this morning; you and your dog were almost killed tonight after finding a dead man earlier this evening and after you were almost killed last night. It's like you're on a mission to investigate all murders that come your way, and you need to stop." He took a step closer and pointed to my shirt. "Before you lose more than just your tassels. And no. That is not a threat. It's common sense that you seem to lack."

Everything had happened so fast that I hadn't had time to think, but his words now had thoughts racing through my head. Could the explosion be related to Ronnie Martin and the fact that we found Dan Martin tonight? It could be. Someone could have watched us from the woods and left before the police arrived. Maybe they knew who we were. But it could also be related to my parents' case. "Has anyone found a note or evidence of foul play near my house? Why do you think the explosion was on purpose?"

"I don't believe in this many coincidences." He looked me in the eye. "Just please stop whatever you're doing and leave investigating to the professionals."

A non-answer, again. Which was an answer. Tito stirred in my arms and sighed. I looked down to see the poor guy was fast asleep. I took a step closer to Mahoney and hissed low. "If you have questions relating to Tessa last night, my house exploding, or finding Dan Martin's body this afternoon, or if you wish to share everything you know about my parents' murders, feel free to reach out. Other than that, I'm not your concern."

Before he could answer, someone cried, "Oh my Lord, no. No!" We turned to see Mr. Leni, our local amateur historian, looking at my house with a shocked expression on his face. Call me naive, but I was compelled to shout, "No one was hurt, Mr. Leni. The fire didn't spread, and as you can see, Tito and I are fine."

"Of course, you're fine!" he scoffed. "This is the Bates-Duma's house, built in 1886, not one of these modern matchstick houses full of synthetic crapola! You would have had seventeen minutes to escape before a house like this burned down." He stared mournfully at the burned interior of the first floor. "Thank goodness it didn't come to that, but they're never the same after a fire." He shuddered. "I guess we should be thankful it didn't reach the Miller-Youngdom house, our region's most prominent example of Eastlake/Queen Anne style. Your house is a brick Victorian vernacular that's common in the district. But it's still a tragedy." He looked back at me, his eyes clearing. "I'm glad no one was hurt. Of course."

Having absolutely nothing to say to that speech, I cleared my throat and murmured, "Of course." Mahoney caught my eye, his own bright with amusement, but I was in no mood to share positive feelings with him, even when a part of me wanted to sit down and laugh until I cried. I looked at my house once again. Maybe I'd just cry.

"Angie!" Anthony's voice suddenly called. Finally! I turned to see a policeman holding him back behind yellow tape. I waved for him to be allowed to come through, and the policeman complied. We ran toward each other, and soon Tito and I were lifted and engulfed in his arms. I never thought I'd feel so grateful to see anyone other than family. Had Anthony become family, somehow? Tito yipped but cuddled back into my arms, tired but watchful, the moment Anthony put me down. "What happened?" he asked, grabbing my shoulders to look me up and down and make sure I was in one piece.

Something made me turn to look at Mahoney, but he was speaking to a group of my neighbors and taking notes. Surely that wasn't a supervisor's job? I wasn't even sure if it fell to the sheriff's office or the police department to investigate.

"We're fine," I answered. With a repressed shudder, I turned to study my house carefully for the first time. Mr. Leni was right. It had good bones.

"Do you think this is related to your parents' case or to Ronnie and Dan Martin?"

"I don't know," I whispered with a shake of my head. Had someone tried to kill me?

"Where will you stay?"

I shrugged. "I could stay with Abuela Luci, but she keeps late hours. A night owl if there ever was one. Plus, I don't want to bring any trouble to her house. The insurance company will probably pay for temporary housing. Can you take me to the Fairfield Inn on Monument?"

"How about you stay with me?" he asked. "The carriage house has two master bedrooms on opposite sides. You'd be close enough to your house to supervise any rebuilding and next to the funeral home for work. I'm almost done setting up every corner of the carriage house and the funeral home with security cameras. I think it's where you would be the safest, especially because I know everything you've been up to."

It was perfect! The only snag was that I wasn't sure if he and I would be compatible as roommates. "I don't think you've thought this through… How about we give it a one-week trial run? For all I know, I snore. No hard feelings if you decide you can't live with me."

It was another half hour before I was free to leave with Anthony. The evidence collected so far, along with my statements, had them predicting it would only take one to two weeks to finish the fire investigation.

"Angie, I know I've asked before, even though it's none of my business, but is there something between you and Brian Mahoney?"

"No." I blew out a breath. "But I can't seem to shake him. And trust me, I've tried." The moment of the explosion came back to me. I looked up at the sky. "Why?"

Anthony must've thought I was talking to him and not the universe because he said, "I just caught a look from him. A jealous boyfriend vibe."

"Does he have any reason not to trust you other than your arrest for criminally trespassing and stealing evidence from the government?"

"I prefer, 'breaking into my ex's office to save a young man's life,' thank you."

"Well? Does he?" I insisted.

Anthony scratched his neck. "I dated his favorite cousin back in college. We were together for a long time, and I grew close to his family. Eventually, I figured out what I wanted out of life and that we weren't compatible, but she felt I had led her on. It's what she told her family, and I understand why she felt that way, but it wasn't true. It took me a while to sort what I wanted from what I thought was expected of me. I don't think Brian has anything against me as a person. Still, he was her shoulder to cry on—he was everyone in his family's shoulder to cry on or lean on—and I think me breaking into a prosecutor's office cemented his opinion that I'm... heedless, I guess."

Everyone's shoulder to cry on. I wanted to know more because his family seemed perfect, but at the same time, I didn't want anything to make Brian Mahoney more human to me. Not until I figured out what he was up to.

But the bit about his favorite cousin got me thinking. "You're not attracted to me, are you? Because that could complicate things." I didn't think he was, but it wouldn't hurt to ask. Our friendship was becoming increasingly important to me.

"You're cute as heck, but I'm not attracted to you in the least." After a moment of hesitation, he explained, "I'm not attracted to anyone in the least. That's what took me a long time to accept about myself. I just don't feel attraction, romantic, sexual, or otherwise." A shrug. "I used to think there was something wrong with me, but there's not. It's just how I'm built. I love and need friendship chemistry, though, and I don't find it often. It's what I had with his cousin, and it's what I have with you." He bumped his shoulder with mine. "How about you? Are you attracted to me?"

I smiled. "You have great arms, and I'm an arm-girl, but they're attached to you, and you feel more like one of my many cousins, so no." I looked up at him. "I do get you, though."

He laughed, crooked his arm around my shoulder, and gave me a quick squeeze. It felt like more than a cousinly hug. It felt like a *brotherly* hug. Tito opened one eye long enough to lick Anthony's hand, and I wondered if he'd been listening. I felt emotional for the first time since I'd hauled myself up after the explosion. "I'm sorry about your parents, Anthony."

"I know you are. You're easy to read. Just don't beat yourself up for not knowing about it. We're still getting to know one another in this strange partnership."

"Are they why you decided to become an attorney?" I asked since he was in this rare, unguarded mood.

"Yes. But not for the reasons you think." He was thoughtful for a moment. "After my parents were killed, I hated the man who got behind the wheel while he was drunk with more passion and emotion than a little human body could hold. But when I saw him in court, he and his family looked more broken than even me or Pappa. It taught me to blame the system that kept putting him in jail and then letting him out because what he needed was a strong rehabilitation program. I became a criminal defense lawyer to try to change things. And on that note," he began as we climbed the steps to the carriage house apartment. "Don't let anyone in here without a warrant."

"Why?" I eyed him suspiciously.

"I've got additional trackers here, and we don't want questions about them, now do we?"

"So, you just have them lying around where anyone can see them?"

He looked heavenward a moment, and it occurred to me he was giving me a place to stay, and I shouldn't be too annoying. "There was a suspicious fire in your house, a murderer almost shot you, and you discovered Dan Martin's body, all in two days! Detectives will want to talk to you in the next couple of days or weeks. They might visit you here. They might want to look around. You won't let them without a warrant. I'll store the trackers elsewhere, but still…"

"You're right." I gave him a sheepish grin as he opened the door.

Anthony offered a tour, but I was too tired and declined. He lent me an oversized t-shirt, I took a shower, and I laid down next to Tito, who was already snoring. I only had two things left to do. First, I texted Nalissa: "My house exploded, and I happened upon a dead man. Tomorrow's looking busy. See you at eleven-thirty or don't bother." If that didn't convince her I had plenty of information to trade, nothing would.

Calling Abuela Luci was next. I hated to worry her yet again. But her reaction when I told her the latest news was surprising. "Well, you certainly lead an exciting life, Angie! And you can tell me all about it over a special ceremony I have planned for us tomorrow. Don't come to me. I'll come to you. I believe that carriage house has a view of both the cemetery and the river, perfect for our purposes." I asked her to please bring any clothes I had at her house over to me in the morning since firefighters hadn't let me go to my bedroom upstairs, and we hung up. It was a good thing she and I had frequent telenovela marathons and sleepovers at her house. I had a closet and chest drawer full of clothes there. One less thing to worry about.

Special ceremonies were now the new thing to worry about, and morning came soon enough...

Tito looked at the vast, grassy cemetery as if it were heaven. So many places to pee. Eager to mark his territory but respectful of final resting places, he couldn't seem to find the right spot. He finally bestowed his precious pee way back near the cemetery's only mausoleum and then led a zombie-like me (I hadn't yet had my coffee) back upstairs.

Anthony had left a note next to a carafe full of piping hot coffee, saying that he had errands to run and wouldn't be back until ten. I sipped at a hot cup nestled appreciatively between my hands as I looked, and Tito sniffed at our surroundings.

The carriage house was set to a right angle about a hundred yards away from the funeral home at the end of the long driveway. The front door was up the stairs on the cemetery side, and it led to a cozy living room with cemetery views. Next to that was a decent-enough kitchen and a small eating area with a river view. The door in the living room led to Anthony's bedroom, and the door in the dining room led to the spare bedroom.

It didn't surprise me that Anthony's bedroom overlooked the cemetery. That meant mine overlooked the river and the city. It pleased me to look out and see the sparkling water and sun shining against the windows of the buildings on the other side of the river. There was a triple garage downstairs, but the hearse and minivan always seemed to be parked along the driveway as far as I had seen. I wondered if it would be all right with Pappa and Anthony to park my dad's car in one of the garages if there was room.

Thoughts of what had happened, whether someone had tried to kill me, and dealing with insurance and rebuilding suddenly overwhelmed me, and I pushed them aside. *Take it one step at a time, Angie. Finish your coffee. If someone is trying to kill you, you're on to something. You simply need to be more aware and alert now.*

Abuela Luci knocked on the door at eight-thirty, a huge, bright red laptop bag slung over her shoulder, a grocery bag with some clothes, and a glint in her dark eyes. "Where is Anthony?" she whispered.

"He's not here."

"How long will we be alone, do you think?"

"About an hour," I estimated, feeling suspicious. A special ceremony, she'd said. I'd had plenty of special teas and readings with Abuela, but never a ceremony. "We have an appointment at eleven-thirty at the funeral home." Providing Nalissa didn't back out again. But with the bait I'd given her, I doubted it.

"We'll be done by then." She slipped by me and went directly to the coffee table in the dining room. "Boy, do I have a treat in store for you!" A chill ran down my spine.

"Sit cross-legged on the other side of the table, please," she instructed as she began fishing items out of her purse, like Mary Poppins. Candles, candle holders, shoes, and clothes. "Can I change first?" I asked. She thought about it. "*Sí.* But be quick about it."

I threw on the skinny jeans and orange t-shirt folded at the top of the pile she'd brought and went back out. "Really? Orange? You know it's not my color. This isn't even mine. And it clashes with my glittery blue nail polish."

"Orange is nobody's color, and how about a thank you?" Abuela Luci said before turning back to Cousin Wanda, whom she was already chatting with on Zoom.

"Thank you," I murmured.

"Hi again, Angie!" Wanda waved, her curls bouncing under her hot pink lace headband. "Three times in twenty-four hours! There's a reason you and I are connecting so much, and I meditated on it this morning." She got closer. "I'm convinced it's all tied to your first spiritual journey." The twinkle in her eyes was only a little less bright than Abuela's glint.

"Oh no," Abuela interrupted. "She's not going on a spiritual journey. I am. I simply need Angie before me because the answers I'm looking for are in her future aura. And you, of course, are here to be my guide."

"Why do you need a guide?" I asked

"To guide me to the answers I'm searching for if I get sidetracked. It's very easy to get sidetracked."

"All right then." I slapped my hands on my thighs. "Let's get this ceremony started!" I got comfortable, feeling a bit more ready for what was to come, and happy to participate in anything that would make Abuela feel better about my mishaps lately. I sniffed the candle. "What herbs are in it? And what are you going to do with it?"

"No herbs. Just cojoba seeds," Abuela answered. "Our Taíno ancestors were the first to discover their powers, you know."

"Cojoba? What's that? I can't have anything funny in here. It wouldn't be fair to Anthony. He's in enough trouble over something else and might be disbarred as it is."

"Don't worry," Wanda said soothingly. "It's just ground seeds from the Cojoba tree in Puerto Rico and candle wax. Perfectly not illegal, and nothing funny about it. The flame helps ground you, and the sweet, earthy scent of the seeds helps you access theta brain waves, which allow the hippocampus to reveal its hidden knowledge. Kind of like how focusing on a swinging pendulum or watch helps create a hypnotic state, and lavender helps slow-wave sleep, or incense eases stress and increases focus.

I groaned because I hadn't had good luck with candles thus far but sat back because I trusted Wanda. It wasn't her fault the universe's plans weren't in sync with my needs.

"Just sit in front of the candle, Angie, so that I can focus on you, too. But don't stare at the flame," Abuela instructed. "Hypnosis is no joke." I took a deep breath and, without meaning to, stared at the flame.

NINE

"The stars advise you but do not oblige you."

SPANISH PROVERB

I snapped to it, feeling happy and relaxed, unaware of how much time had passed. I looked to Abuela and gasped. "Abuela! Your eyes are outlined in layers of fluorescent green!"

Abuela stared back and exclaimed, "Oh Angie, what a wonderful aura you will have!" And then she froze.

"What's up with Abuela Luci?" I asked Wanda, not at all worried but curious.

"She's in a hypnotic state. From what she said, I believe a picture of your future aura is now before her, and she's reading it. Today, her intent was quite clear, and her temporal lobe has taken over. However, you had no intent, so your subconscious yearnings took charge. I'm guessing you can see fluorescent green layers around Luci's eyes because you yearned to see other people's spiritual gifts. Luci can see auras and do readings based on them, and that's what you're seeing highlighted in her."

"Is that why you have a fluorescent green flame in the middle of your forehead?" I asked, staring at the flickering flame. "Because you read fire?"

She smiled. "Something like that."

A warm sensation came over me, and a moment later, a deep appreciation for the coffee table. "Look at it, Wanda. Can You see it? It's made of oak." I ran a hand over it. "It was once a part of the forest." I got up and waltzed over to the window overlooking the cemetery. "They're all a part of me," I said, my eyes sweeping across every grave. I skipped over to the other window. "And the river and all the little guppies inside!" Across the river, there were windows. So many windows. "My brothers and sisters across the river are working and feeling and loving and despairing in those buildings. We're all connected. We are all one! I guess I needed to see it. Why have we never done this before?" And that gave me a thought. "I'll be right back!"

I ran off to the bathroom and looked in the mirror. "Oh my." There was a fluorescent ear hovering above my head. A third ear. I had heard of a third eye but never a third ear. "This is why I can hear dead people," I said to the mirror as I traced my green lobe.

I couldn't see any other gifts on my face, so I looked at my arms and hands and then gasped at my bare feet. "I have a fluorescent green left toe! What does that mean? What can it do?"

"What's that?" Wanda called from the laptop in the living room as I wiggled my toe up and down, left and right.

"Nothing!" I tried squeezing my toe. Nothing. Then I wondered if I had any other fluorescent green glows on me. I tried to look at my backside and went around in circles, like Tito chasing his tail, but I couldn't find anything else after a thorough search, including stripping. Wanda kept calling from the living room, and I quickly dressed and returned.

"How many gifts are there in the universe?" I asked when I got back. I couldn't tell her about my third ear and green left toe, even though I was dying to know what my left toe could do, because I couldn't ask her to keep a secret from Abuela Luci. There was too much warmth and love in me to ask any living being to do something against their nature.

"I once read that only 0.000013 percent of the population has gifts, and there are some strange ones out there. I grew up with a girl whose grandmother could talk to alpacas, and she only found out because she went to an alpaca farm back when that was a thing. Can you imagine? If she had never gone to an alpaca farm, she never would have known she had the gift of speaking to them!"

A knock on the door made us both jump. It couldn't be Anthony because he had a key. Did Pappa have a key? I ran to check if it was him. "Oh!" I said when I peered through the peephole. "It's Lieutenant Mahoney from last night! And he has a lovely fluorescent green mohawk!"

"Lieutenant? And he has a gift? Angie, get back here and do not open that door!" Wanda hissed from the screen.

"Why ever not?" I ran back and kneeled before her. "He's part of the 0.000013% of the population with a gift. Doesn't he deserve to know? And also, when he looks at me, I get a funny warmth in the pit of my stomach, and it spreads to all of my limbs. I usually resist it, but today I think I would like to explore it."

Another knock. "Angie? We need to talk," Mahoney called.

Wanda got so close to the camera I could see her tiny pores. "You have lovely skin. What do you use?" I asked her.

"Goat's milk soap. I make it myself. Now listen to me," she half-whispered. "Your grandmother is in a trance, there's a strange scent in your home, *and now there's a policeman on the other side of that door*! You cannot let him in!"

"But you said this is perfectly legal."

"It *is* perfectly legal, but it looks and smells strange. He'll naturally ask questions, and you're very open right now. You might tell him things you wouldn't normally want to, and you'll be contending with this unknown gift he has."

"Um. All right." I skipped back to the door. "I can't open the door, Brian." I tilted my head to the side and put my hand on the door. "Is it all right if I call you Brian?"

"Sure. But why can't you open the door?"

"Because... you don't have a warrant," I said triumphantly, remembering what Anthony had said.

"Why do I need a warrant if I just want to talk to you?" Over at the coffee table, I saw Wanda put her hands to her face. Maybe I shouldn't have mentioned a warrant?

"I'm just being friendly and kidding. Hahahahaha." I tried to think but found it challenging. My heart felt open, and I didn't want to lie. I wanted to open the door, jab at his florescent green mohawk, and ask him if he was a good person or a bad person.

But something started to poke at my brain. It wasn't pleasant, like the warmth in my heart. "Why do you want to talk to me?"

Silence. A restrained sigh. And then, "Because the flowers on Dan Martin's desk were devil's breath." Wanda gasped. Which made me gasp, even though I had no idea what that was. "Everyone exposed to it last night has had a headache, felt dizzy, and gotten nausea," Brian continued. "Thankfully, no one was exposed for a prolonged period, and they're all fine this morning. I checked in on Pappa, and he said he's feeling great, but he said that both you and he had symptoms yesterday. Between the devil's breath and the fire at your house, I wanted to check in on you."

"Aw. You're worried about me?"

"It's my job, Angie." The unpleasant poke came back, this time in the middle of my forehead. Was that where the hippocampus was located? I rubbed at it, not ready to be pulled out of my idyllic state. "But yes, I'm worried about you. I can't seem to stop worrying about you." His tone was one of reluctant honesty. I looked through the peephole again. His forehead was pressed to the door.

Without conscious thought, I floated my forehead down to the door as well. "So…are you saying you care?"

Pause. "I care."

I closed my eyes. "I believe you, but I don't want to believe you." It's like I'd lost control of my tongue. It was loose, like my thoughts and feelings. "Something tugs me toward you, and then… something else pulls me away." I looked through the peephole again to see bright blue eyes staring speculatively at the door. Then, he was smiling. His real smile. Had I said something to make him happy?

"Angie," Abuela called. I turned to see her wearing a beatific grin. She was about to say something else, but Wanda shushed her.

"I didn't know you had company," Brian said.

"Abuela's here."

"I have something else to ask you. Is that okay?" he asked in a low voice.

"Uh, sure."

"Are you aware that your car was completely out of gas?"

I scratched my head. Why was he checking on my car? Was it part of the investigation into the explosion at my house? "I thought I had filled it up, but it wouldn't turn on yesterday morning, and the needle pointed toward empty, so I walked. Why?"

"It looks like someone emptied it. Someone wanted you to walk. Remember the Altima?"

"Oh. Um, yeah." I didn't want Abuela to hear this, not when she seemed to be in a blissful state. I looked back, and she and Wanda were whispering. "But I can't talk about this right now."

He sighed deeply. "Well, I'm glad you're not alone. I'm even glad you're staying with Anthony. Take care, and don't forget you have my number. I'll catch you later."

"You're frowning," Wanda observed to me a moment later. "That means you're starting to cross back to our shared plane."

I looked out both windows. The cemetery's grass was too dry and the river too low. Which reminded me, when was it going to rain? "What plane was I just in?" I asked.

"I'm glad you asked!" Wanda exclaimed, clapping her hands together in glee. "You've never expressed an interest before, and it has greatly concerned most of your ascendants. Except for Mama Juana."

"Who's Mama Juana?"

Wanda and Abuela Luci shared a smile, and then Abuela continued as if I hadn't asked anything. "There are seven planes of existence. Different cultures call them different things, but here they are commonly known as the physical, astral, mental, spiritual, consciousness, logic, and monadic."

Wanda nodded. "And you were in the highest subplane of the third lowest plane."

I shook my head. "This is too complicated for me right now."

"I give a class every Wednesday from six to eight. Maybe *you should come*," Abuela said with the pointed look of a grandmother who'd been telling her granddaughter the same thing for two years.

I threw up my hands. "Stop guilting me! You know that's when I teach art at the senior center."

She crossed her arms. "Of course. You conveniently started giving that class the same week I started giving my class and asked you to be my assistant. I had matching outfits for us and everything."

"It's a grant, Abuela, and I have no control over the schedule."

"Welp, we are definitely in the lowest step of the physical planes now," Wanda tsked. Abuela narrowed her eyes at her and shut the laptop. "What's this Wanda was telling me about you sniffing Devil's Breath?"

"I didn't sniff anything, Abuela. I was in the same room with the flowers, and it gave me a headache, but I'm fine. Tell me what you know about it."

"It's a powerful plant originally from South American countries and is legal to grow here. It puts victims into a compliant trance. Almost like they're devoid of their own free will. A large dose can kill you. Where did you say you came across it, exactly?"

"It was in a vase in a client's study."

"Well. Now that you know what it looks like, you can stay away from it."

A jiggle at the door had us looking back. A moment later, Anthony walked in.

"Anthony! Where have you been, roomie?" I saw Abuela quickly blow out the candles out of the corner of my eye.

"Am I interrupting something?"

"No. *Nada*." Abuela smiled.

He eyed us suspiciously for another moment before giving me a significant look. "Our eleven-thirty appointment is early."

Nalissa! Of course, she was early. Probably some other psychological power move on her part to make us scramble. She was good.

I turned to Abuela, feeling torn because I knew Abuela was concerned for me, and I didn't want to hurry her out the door. She surprised me by giving me the same beatific smile she'd worn when she'd been in the highest subplanes of the third lowest plane. "Go and take care of your needs. I won't stop you."

I nodded. Though I didn't fully understand what had happened in the last half-hour with the candles and bliss, I knew by Abuela's calm demeanor that she would be all right. We went down to the driveway together, where Abuela's Kia Soul, Nalissa's van, and a late model dark grey Acura TLX with tinted windows were parked. Abuela pulled out with a wave.

"Yours?" I motioned to the Acura. Anthony nodded. "Where's Nalissa?" I asked the moment Abuela left.

"In Pappa's office." He opened the prep room through the back and glanced back at me. "Orange is not your color. I say this as a friend."

"Orange is nobody's color. Did Pappa tell you about the Devil's Breath?"

"Mahoney called him, and we looked it up. It's a powerful, sedative plant that robs people of their free will." He shook his head. "Crazy stuff."

I nodded. "It got me thinking…What if the plant was used on Ronnie to get him to take his own life?"

Anthony looked down at the ground for a long moment. "It seems crazy and far-fetched, but no crazier than Tilly Sandberg being replaced by her long-lost twin." He looked at me. "The fact that the flowers were in Dan Martin's study would also tie into our theory that the scene was set last night to do whatever was done to Ronnie, to him."

We were quiet as we both considered this. A moment later, I shook the thought off. "The police know about it. As Pappa said, we can leave it all to them for now. Let's focus on Nalissa and what she knows about my parents."

"Wait." He held me back. "We can't tell her about the tracker. It's the one thing that could get us in trouble, and we can't give her anything to use against us."

With that, he led me up the stairs, and we walked in to see Nalissa and Pappa chatting about security cameras. She finished her sentence and turned to smile at me. "You've been leading an interesting life lately."

"So have you." I didn't smile back. This was about my parents. She had information, and I *needed* it. "Let's chat."

TEN

"Start with Sunday." I pulled the spare chair forward, sat down, and crossed my arms and legs. "Where were you mugged?"

She gave me a slight nod, acknowledging I held the upper hand. "Pappa dropped me off at my car when we left the Carlson's. I stopped at my office to change and then went home. A burly male, about six foot two inches tall, jumped me from behind at my front door. He put me in a chokehold, dipped into my bag, and took my phone. *Only* my phone—not my bag or even my wallet." She looked at us, in turn, to make sure we understood it wasn't a regular mugging. "He then threw me to the floor and ran off, and I couldn't get a close look because my security cameras had been disabled."

She took a deep breath as if gearing up to say more, but I interrupted her. "Were you hurt?"

"It's not the first time I've been put in a chokehold," she replied with a shrug.

"And your attacker didn't say anything?" Anthony asked.

"No, but—"

"Wait." Pappa stood up, a frown on his face. "You're saying the attacker was after the pictures you took of that collage, the ones that showed Lillian Carlson was the woman sitting next to Angie's mom during that dinner twelve years ago. But that would mean you and Angie were being watched, and you were recognized even though you were wearing an excellent disguise, and then they waited for you at your house to mug you and take your phone… *Or* it could mean that you and I were followed on our way to your car, but I was watchful before you jumped inside the hearse, and I didn't see anyone inside the cars parked on the street near the Carlson's except for Anthony."

Anthony nodded in agreement. "It's a cul de sac on a long street. I watched as you left, and there were no other movements or lights."

"Maybe the mugging is about another article you're working on?" Pappa suggested.

Nalissa treated us to an exasperated look. "If you all would let me finish, I was about to say that they also broke into my house but only took my laptop and a recorder. My best guess is they wanted to see if I keep anything there, like how much I know about Angie's parents' case, or maybe even something to use to blackmail me into staying silent. But I automatically upload everything to my cloud, and I don't keep anything sensitive anywhere. And all my passwords are complex and up here," she tapped her head. "That's why I was able to send Angie the pictures of her mom and Lillian as soon as I got hold of a computer. And it can only be about Angie's parents' case because the only two articles I'm currently working on are puff pieces."

I thought back to the night of the Gala, picked through every memory…and realized I was to blame. "Oh no," I said, closing my eyes a moment. "I yelled your name when I heard you screaming in my earpiece. Nalissa is a rare name, and you're known locally." I sunk into my chair, my heart sinking with me. Nalissa could have been hurt. "If they realized you took pictures of their anniversary collage and that you used your phone to do so, it means the inside of the house was being monitored. You escaped, but me saying your name gave you away. That's why someone was waiting to steal your phone when you got home." I looked up at her. "We may be onto Lillian as the false witness, but now she and Neil are onto you. Because of me."

"They're onto you, too," she reminded me.

"Of course. But everyone knows that I've never stopped looking into my parents' case. In a way, the fact that I'm their daughter protects me. If anything happens to me, too many people would think it was too much of a coincidence, and they'd demand a new investigation."

Nalissa shrugged one shoulder. "I should've known they would have every room watched during a large event at their house. The moment a security camera caught me taking pictures, they might have questioned the caterer, who had no incentive to hide my real name. That may be how they got it. So don't feel guilty for yelling my name. You're new at this. I'm not."

Anthony pushed off the hutch he'd been leaning against. "I'm sorry you were attacked, Nalissa, but it's another good reason for us to partner. It's time to tell us everything you know about Angie's parents. The sooner it's solved, the sooner you're safe."

"Very well." She stood up and tugged on her white linen blazer, and I straightened. "The deal you proposed was that we collaborate on murder cases that come our way. I know you have two new ones. If I find this isn't a two-way street, I'm backing up." She held her hand out. First me, then Pappa, and finally Anthony shook it. With a steady look into my eyes, she said, "Brace yourself." I did. "When Angie came to me six months ago to ask me to investigate her parents' case, I tried to dismiss it as not worthy of my time, but it lingered in my mind and wouldn't leave me alone. A few weeks ago, I decided to do a little digging to put my mind to rest. I started with Craig Fisher, the CEO of Sonrad." She looked at me directly, and I went cold. Craig Fisher. Again. Could he have been the key all along, looking after me throughout the years and pretending he cared only to see what I knew and what I was up to? "Did you ever ask him what your parents were *really* working on at the base?"

I nodded vigorously. "Many times. I begged, in fact, but I always got the same answer. My dad didn't work at the base, and my mom was working on new adaptive sonar and radar systems technology. I didn't believe him, but I also knew he couldn't tell me anyway because he has a top security clearance, and whatever they were working on was likely classified. I asked him again and again because I had to try. I couldn't give up." I waited for Nalissa to continue. When she simply watched me, as if she was expecting more, I added, "But Craig Fisher was away on business the night my parents died, and he seemed genuinely devastated at the funeral. My grandmother would've noticed and said something if she thought he was faking it."

Nalissa tilted her head. "I got the same answer and the same impression that he was still very much saddened by what happened. But a few weeks after I spoke with him, I received a call from his soon-to-be ex-wife, Jessica. Craig has a maid and a part-time cook, and both are spying on him for her. They told her I dropped by, she called me, and became my second source." She paused and regarded me again. "What she said might be hard to hear."

"Just say it. Please." My voice was steady, but my heart was out of control.

Nalissa's eyes didn't leave mine. "She told me that detectives questioned Craig when he got back to town the day after your parents were shot, which he expected because he employed your mom. He was cooperative. But a few days later, while he and Jessica were having breakfast, he came across an article where your suspicions about the amber pendant your father was wearing were mentioned, and he was stunned, but he wouldn't say why. One of the detectives came back the next evening, and Craig led him to his study. Jessica thought Craig had called the detective back because the article about the amber pendant jogged something in his memory, and she was resentful that he hadn't shared anything with her when she asked. Typical of him, she said. So, she went to her craft room above the study, where she knew she could hear some of what went on in there through a vent. She wanted to see if anything Craig said jostled her memory as well." Nalissa rolled her eyes at this, but I motioned for her to get on with it.

"Keep in mind that Jessica didn't catch everything that was said and that it was twelve years ago. She can't remember the exact words, but she's quite clear on the impression she got because it shocked her, and she thinks about it often." When she saw I was ready to shake her, she rushed on. "Craig and the detective seemed to be plotting to get some woman to say that your mom had been bragging about a necklace she'd be wearing the night of the reception so that there would be both a motive and an explanation for you saying that your father's amber pendant was missing. She didn't catch who the woman would be, but she did hear that the woman had been sitting next to your mom at a dinner party the Saturday before your parents were killed." She let that sink in before continuing. "Jessica had been at the Carlson's tenth-anniversary party and had chatted with your parents there, so she knew that was the dinner party they were talking about, but she couldn't remember who had been sitting next to your mom."

The question utmost on my mind was, "Who was the detective Craig spoke to?"

At that exact moment, Anthony asked, "Does Jessica think Craig was involved in the murders?"

Nalissa shook her head at Anthony. "That evening in his study, Craig kept whining that he had nothing to do with the murders. He would never have wished anything bad on your parents, but he couldn't lose his position over *loose lips*. He was distressed, but the detective didn't seem to care. He advised Craig not to let their false witness know that the Air Force Office of Special Investigations was taking over the case. Two days later, Jessica discovered ten grand missing from one of his accounts. One he didn't know she had access to."

I sprang up and put a hand to my head. My mind was pulling me in three different directions, and I didn't know which one to follow first.

"Why did Jessica Fisher wait this long to say something?" Pappa asked.

"She didn't think Craig was responsible for the murders, and she wanted to protect him. But she caught Craig cheating on her, and she now suspects it wasn't the first time. She says she's tired of being naïve."

"Who was the detective?" I demanded again.

She took a deep breath and let it out. "It was Lieutenant Steven Webber, now Captain Webber." A pause. "And Jessica doesn't know if the ten grand went to Webber or the false witness. But my bet is on Webber. Just instinct from things that haven't added up with him over the years."

A bitter taste filled my mouth, and I couldn't wait to see Webber again. I bunched my fist. "I've always known I couldn't trust him."

Pappa also looked angry. He narrowed his eyes at Nalissa. "Who's your source at the sheriff's office? Have you told them about Webber? Why haven't they reported him?"

Nalissa shook her head. "I'm sorry, but that's the one thing I can't tell you." Pappa and Anthony exchanged a glance, and Nalissa sighed. "I have a deal with them, same as I have a deal with you. I can't and won't betray anyone I have a deal with. Otherwise, none of this works."

Pappa and Anthony saw the truth of this and backed off. We were all quiet for a moment. The information about Webber was new and a lot to take in.

I walked to the window that overlooked the front parking lot. "I need to get all of this straight." I pressed my head to the cool glass to help me get a grip on it all and sift through theories I had thought up throughout the years, even when I didn't have any names. After a moment, I turned to them. "I must've been right about the murderers being after the amber if reading about the pendant in the newspaper made Craig Fisher freak out. It sounds like he let something about the amber stones slip to someone; he guessed his *loose lips* led to the murders, and he knew he could get in trouble, especially since it was all classified information. He got Lillian to lie about my mom bragging about a necklace to give the murderers a motive the police could latch onto and maybe even to confuse matters if anyone believed me that my dad had a missing pendant. And he might have paid Webber to squash talk about my dad's amber and instead focus on my mom's supposed necklace. But how did he get Lillian to cooperate? And was Webber known to be on the take? How would someone like Craig even know something like that?"

"I don't know," Nalissa mused. "Everything you say makes sense, and it fits, but it's also conjecture upon conjecture."

"It may be conjecture, but it's based on years of thinking about all of this and coming up with theories. Putting new pieces of information together with workable theories is easier for me than for you."

Nalissa tilted her head as if conceding the point. "Then share your old theories."

I looked at her. "My main theory has always been out there. The amber stones were on a ship rumored to have Ponce de Leon's fountain of youth, and I've always believed that's why they were studying them at the base. The questions I need to be answered are why my dad felt the need to keep one on him, who found out they were important enough to commit murder over, and how."

Nalissa sat back down and crossed her legs. "You told me that six months ago, and you know I need more. Come on. It's your turn."

I nodded. A deal was a deal. And I'd gotten more than I expected out of Nalissa. My heart was pounding at how everything was coming together. But I knew I had to be cautious and not get ahead of myself or latch onto an idea so much that I lost sight of other possibilities. There was still a lot to confirm, and there were new leads to follow. I turned to Anthony. "Tell her what we've been up to. I need time to think."

Anthony took the chair I had vacated earlier and sat down in front of Nalissa. "We followed Lillian to Craig Fisher's house yesterday, and she didn't take her regular car. She took a Jeep Cherokee. Craig answered, and they went inside. A short time later, they came out and argued on his front porch. Angie snuck through the woods to get close, but she couldn't hear them."

Nalissa's eyes widened. "So, days after we're caught taking pictures of that anniversary dinner, Lillian goes off to Craig Fisher's house in a car she doesn't normally use, and they argue..." She looked excited. "The evidence is stacking up that she's our false witness. She must suspect we're onto her because of the pictures we took, and if she argued with Craig immediately after she found out what we were up to, it gives proof to what Jessica said—that it was Craig who directed her to lie to the police. We need to figure out what he had over her to make her commit perjury."

"Maybe they were having an affair back then, and he threatened her with telling Neil," Anthony suggested.

Pappa shook his head. "But then Lillian could have also threatened him with telling Jessica. They'd be at a standstill."

As they continued to throw and discard theories, my mind settled enough to sort through all the new information. One old theory began fluttering around, landing on fact upon fact for short moments, showing me how it could fit. "I have some thoughts," I finally said, interrupting them. "What if Lillian was the person Craig loosened his lips to in the first place? Maybe they *were* having an affair, and he let slip classified information about the amber stones. Then, after the murders, with me mentioning the missing amber stone pendant in the newspaper, Craig put one and one together and suspected that Lillian had leaked the information to the wrong people. If he confronted her, and she knew that it could be traced back to her, that would be her motive to feed the police false information. She might even have been the person to tell Craig that Captain Webber was on the take and could help them."

Nalissa raised one eyebrow. "I don't know. That's quite a leap."

"Not really..." Anthony began, and I could see the wheels turning in his head. "The night of the Gala, we learned that Tilly Sandberg—the real Tilly—used to call Lillian honeytrap," he reminded her. "Honeytrap is usually a term for a beautiful woman used to lure men. I thought it was an insult at the time, but what if Lillian *is* a honeytrap? And Tilly knew? We know Tilly had something over her, too. It sounds stranger than fiction, but as they say, the truth often is."

Pappa slowly nodded. "Wright Patterson Air Force Base is one of the country's largest and most important bases. Air Force Research Laboratories is based there. I've had a few clients over the years who worked there in high-level roles, and when their loved ones reminisce, they mention how the client used to be worried about espionage."

Nalissa blinked. "That's true. Even low-level workers are routinely reminded spies could target them." She abruptly stood up. "And ever since they married, Lillian Carlson is celebrated for supporting STEM education in schools, which, now that I think on it, doesn't fit anything else they do. But every time she holds one of those fundraisers to give money to schools, she invites plenty of top people from the base and important contractors, like Craig Fisher…"

Pappa spoke excitedly. "She started off doing hair, had an affair with Jessup Sandberg—the owner of the building she worked in and was then introduced by him to Neil—one of Dayton's most powerful men. She married Neil and began to host fundraisers that attract military personnel."

"Wait, how do you know she had an affair with Jessup Sandberg?" Nalissa asked.

Pappa shot me a guilty look, and Nalissa's eyes narrowed.

"We're not keeping anything from you, but we can't reveal the source," I explained. I didn't want to betray Brenda's or Nalissa's trust, so I chose my words carefully. "We learned that Lillian had an affair with Jessup Sandberg. Tilly Sandberg hired a private detective to follow Lillian when she found out, and after that, she seemed to be holding something over Lillian's head. She also called Jessup Sandberg a *mark*. That, and calling Lillian *honeytrap*, fits into our latest theory."

Nalissa accepted this, and we were quiet for a long time, each likely grappling with how far-fetched it all sounded while knowing it was all possible. Anthony eventually took out his phone, and something in his expression changed. He met my eyes, and I instantly knew. The Jeep was on the move.

I cleared my throat. "I think we've gotten as far as we're going to get today. I'm struggling with how crazy it sounds, and I need to let it all settle." I turned to Anthony. "I need to buy some food, treats, and toys for Tito. Do you mind taking me?"

"Sure thing." He moved toward the door, and I followed.

"Not so fast." Nalissa stood in my path with her arms crossed. "I told you everything I know, and you have to admit it has helped immensely. It's your turn to spill on Dan and Ronald Martin and the explosion in your house last night."

Pappa caught my eye. "I know everything she knows, and I can walk you through it. It'll probably be more effective if it's just you and me. We've all been talking over each other."

Nalissa narrowed her eyes at Anthony and me. "I don't think so. There's something you're not telling me."

My mind raced through the last two days for something to give her, to throw her off our scent for now. Mahoney's visit came to mind, and with it, a realization. "Actually, there's something I haven't told any of you. My car wouldn't start yesterday, which is why I walked. With everything going on, I didn't really think about it, not even when I was followed. But Lieutenant Mahoney told me this morning that there was no gas in my car—as in zero, zip, zilch, nada, even though I filled it up recently. I think whoever followed me yesterday morning emptied it. They meant for me to walk."

"You were followed?" Nalissa repeated.

"By a white Altima with tinted windows," I added because if the car was familiar to her, I wanted to know now. She studied me in a way I couldn't interpret before smiling and waving me off. "Off you go, then. I'm sure you need toiletries and such. Pappa will fill me in." I knew what she was doing—acting ambiguous because she knew we were keeping something from her and now wanted us to think she might know something about a white Altima. And damn it, it was working. She was good. We engaged in a staring contest until Anthony thankfully pulled me away.

"The Jeep is at Performance Place," he said as soon as we were out of earshot. "We saw Lillian there when we visited Brenda, remember?"

"Of course I do!" I said as I jogged to his car. "Let's go!"

ELEVEN

"To retire is not to flee, and there is no wisdom in waiting when danger outweighs hope, and it is the part of wise men to preserve themselves today for tomorrow and not risk all in one day."

MIGUEL DE CERVANTES SAAVEDRA,
DON QUIXOTE

"Wait." Anthony dug into a brown paper bag in his trunk and took out a transparent, gray-streaked rectangular sticker. I shifted from one leg to the other as I watched him peel it off its backing and smooth it over the license plate of his Acura. It obscured the numbers by making them look dirty. "I also have my beater college car in the garage, but I think this one will fit in when we park in front of the Schuster," he explained.

"What other magic tricks do you have in that bag?" I asked as I got into the passenger seat.

"I'll tell you along the way."

Five minutes later, we were parked on the other side of the street from the Schuster, a few cars down from Performance Place. Anthony cranked the windows down a nudge and turned the car off. "I don't want a running engine to call attention to us," he explained. The tinted windows helped ward off the hot August sun, but the air was stale and humid, and there was no breeze. "If it gets too hot, I'll turn the air on."

"I'm from Puerto Rico, remember? I can take it." He smiled. I looked through the side-view mirror and asked, "How long has she been here?"

"About thirty minutes, and there's no telling how long she'll stay, so let's settle in."

"Sounds like you've done this before."

"I have, but I missed things I should've seen."

"Were you alone?"

"Yeah."

I squeezed his hand. "Well, now there are two of us." It wasn't unlike me to offer comfort, but it was unlike me to seek it, and I realized that's what I was doing. The realization made me remove my hand and focus instead on watching the door to the building. "Brenda said she didn't want to be involved, but she's the best person to ask if she's ever seen Lillian in here."

He glanced from the rearview mirror to me. "I thought about that, but it's not a good idea."

"Why?"

"If there's one thing I've learned, it's not to burn bridges. Don't ask her so soon after you promised to leave her alone."

I took a deep breath, feeling frustrated but wanting to keep a clear head. "How about you check property records to see who lives or has offices at Performance Place while I keep a lookout?"

Anthony's eyes brightened. "Great idea. I'll focus on residents on the ninth floor. That's where the elevator stopped when we ran into her the day we stopped by Brenda's to get Tilly Sandberg's clothes and photos for the funeral service." He lifted his phone.

The process took over half an hour because he Googled every name that appeared on the property records website. I was so afraid I'd miss Lillian when she stepped or drove out that I kept my eyes on the building and barely blinked. Out of nowhere, I wondered if Brian Mahoney ever went on stakeouts and whether he was lonely when he did.

"A lawyer, a property management firm owner, a broker, and the mysterious Polar Moth Corp we can't find anything on," Anthony repeated. "Those are the ninth-floor residents."

"The Arts Council is a few floors below, too. She's probably a part of it, and they could be having a meeting. Performance Place doesn't exactly scream *seedy meeting place for co-conspirators*, and we have no evidence she's on the ninth floor again." I sighed.

Anthony shifted in his seat to look at me. "She might very well be doing something innocuous. Hell, she might even take the Jeep out for a spin every so often just because. But I think this is a good use of our time. It's noon on a Monday. Most people, no matter how wealthy they are, are working. I don't think there's a meeting of the Arts Council going on, and I doubt she'd make a house visit to her broker or lawyer or property manager, especially in her least-expensive car. She likely doesn't want anyone telling Neil where they saw her car."

My mood lightened. "True. She's less recognizable in the Jeep, and if anyone did see her, it would be easier for her to explain being here than in a roadside motel—" I grabbed his arm. "There she is!" Lillian was driving out of the garage, wearing dark sunglasses, a white shirt, and a dark blazer. I glanced at the digital clock on the interface. 12:03.

"Let's follow her." He turned the car on, but I grabbed his arm.

"No. We're tracking her and will know where she goes. Let's see if anyone else comes out of the building."

Ten minutes later, no one had come out.

"She's turning into her driveway," Anthony, who was looking at the tracking app, said. "What do you want to do?"

"Let me think…" My kitchen had exploded the night before, and I hadn't even had time to sit down and think about what it meant. I didn't even know if it was safe to go back and try to salvage as many of my possessions as I could. The fire had been confined to the kitchen, but there had been a lot of smoke.

My thoughts were interrupted by the sight of a tall, lean, good-looking blond male walking out of Performance Place. I slapped Anthony's arm and dug my nails into his arm. "Him! That guy. I know him!"

He looked through the side view mirror on the driver's side. "The guy who just came out of the building?"

"Yes! We need to follow him!"

Anthony pressed the ignition button while we watched the man's movements. "Why? Where do you know him from?"

"He was in one of Lillian and Neal Carlson's tenth-anniversary party pictures. I noticed him because he was off to the side, smirking at them. Maybe it's nothing, but if he was there, he must know one of them, and now he's walking out of the building minutes after Lillian."

Anthony lengthened his back to get a better look through the rearview mirror. "And you're sure it's the man in the picture?"

I nodded. "Blond, wavy hair. Oblong face. Forehead and high, perfect cheekbones about the same width. Prominent eyes. A slightly rounded chin added to his beauty by keeping him from looking overly masculine. I'd be drawn to him if I hadn't seen the evil smirk. He had presence."

He laughed. "Do you analyze all men this way?"

I smiled. "Not out loud. I was told by middle school friends that it took the fun out of mooning over our crushes." I tilted my head and turned serious. "When a face seizes and then holds my attention, whether in real life, on a screen, or on paper, I study it to learn the technique. Not just a man's face. Any face."

Anthony continued to follow the man's movements. "He's crossing the street. Good. We'll be facing the same direction. And…now he's getting into that blue car in front of the pizza place." He narrated as if I wasn't observing, too.

"It's a VW Passat. If we're going to spy on people, you'll have to learn your cars," I chided.

"That's what I have you for. That and hearing a dead person's last words." The VW drove past us. "I'm going to give him a three-car lead."

"Is there any way we can look up the license plate to see whom it belongs to?" I asked when he pulled out.

"Only if you have other info, like the owner's social security number."

"Do you have any contacts from your old life who can run plates for you?"

He shook his head. "Public defenders and pro bono lawyers don't have those types of contacts."

I took a pen from the center console and wrote the license plate number on the back of a receipt before sticking it in my pocket. "Nalissa probably knows someone who'd run them. If following this guy turns up anything, we may have to ask her for help," I said with a sigh before picking up the burner phone we were using to track Lillian. "Lillian is at her house. Or at least the Jeep is."

"She was at Performance Place for a little over two hours. When we figure out Mr. Pretty's destination, maybe we can come back and question the doorman here."

"Mr. Pretty? Is that what we're calling him?"

"Beats guy with oblong, nearly symmetrical face except for charming, slightly rounded chin."

"You forgot the evil smirk."

He glanced over at me. "I smirk all the time. Did you think mine was evil before you got to know me?"

"No. I thought and still think yours was cynical. It shows you're distrustful. Mr. Pretty's smirk made an otherwise compelling gaze look...purely calculating."

"His gaze is compelling now, too?" Anthony laughed again and shook his head. "All this, and he was barely in the picture."

I smiled, and my chest unexpectedly filled with warmth. It had been a long time since I'd had this camaraderie with someone outside my family. Probably since I'd been a middle school girl giggling over crushes. Abuela Nydia said I had kept new people out because I didn't want to lose anyone else after losing my parents.

The idea that I had wasted years that my parents would have wanted me to live fully tugged at me, but I held it at bay. Helping Anthony stay a few cars behind Mr. Pretty was my priority.

We were right behind him when we followed him into Wright State University. Suddenly, that compelling gaze snapped up to his rearview mirror and looked back at us. Anthony hissed. "He's staring."

"Let's park," I said and tried to act normal.

"No. The sun is in front of him, and our windows are tinted. He can't see us well enough to identify us, but he might have noticed the same car has been behind him for fifteen minutes. Downtown to Wright State is a common enough route. Parking right after we catch him looking would be an amateur move."

I let out a calming breath. "Right. And for all we know, him being at Performance Place just now, and in the anniversary picture, is just a coincidence. There's nothing to fear."

"Yet."

"Right. Yet."

He turned right, and we decided to park. A few minutes later, we pulled out and inched forward until we saw Mr. Pretty enter the building, a briefcase in his hand. He glanced at his watch before picking up the pace. His car was parked in the staff parking lot.

Anthony turned to me. "You look like you could still be in college. Ask those students over there if they know who he is. He seemed like he was late for something, so I don't think there's any danger he'll walk out and see you. But be quick."

I looked at the group of three young women he was talking about. They each had a combination of books, notebooks, and bags. "Do you have anything in here that I could carry other than a brown paper bag full of spy gear?"

Anthony leaned back, rifled along the back seat, and pulled up a worn leather messenger bag. "Perfect." I pulled my hair up into a ponytail with my ever-present scrunchie and pulled my sunglasses down from my head.

"Hey," I said as I walked up to the group. "Hey," one answered with friendly interest. The second one lifted her head in acknowledgment, and the third mumbled a greeting but kept her nose glued to her phone.

"Um, so I know this will sound strange, but…" I took a deep breath and blew it out as if I were embarrassed. "Do you guys know the name of the professor who just walked in? Because if he's a professor here, I definitely want to take his class."

"Mm." The friendly first girl bit her lip. "I know what you mean. He looks like that vampire."

"Vampire?" I repeated.

The second girl stifled a sigh. "I'm so sick of vampires." She side-eyed me. "And women who choose classes based on a professor's looks."

I blushed, despite myself.

"He was an FBI agent, too, a few years back." The third girl looked up from her phone.

"A vampire and FBI agent," I repeated. The conversation was getting away from me.

"He looks like an actor who has played both a vampire and an FBI agent," the second girl explained as if I were hard of hearing.

"I can't remember his name, but he has a British accent," the first girl added.

"The actor or the professor?"

The first girl sighed dreamily. "Both." She gave me a conspiratorial wink, and I could tell she was putting on a show to bate the second girl.

"Mm," I said, smiling and following her lead. Not that I disagreed with the second girl about choosing professors based on their looks, but at least this first girl was being friendly and not judging me. "What about the professor's name?" I tried again.

The second girl seemed done with it all. "Professor Van Chapman. I took Global Encounters with him. It was a waste of time for me, but it might not be for you."

"Is Van his first name or part of his last name?"

"First name." She gave me a curious look as if she couldn't believe I was this interested in the professor. "What are you majoring in?" she asked.

"Art, with a concentration in sculpting." I had acquaintances who had gone to Wright State for their Bachelor of Fine Arts degrees, so I knew enough to answer a few questions, but it was clearly time to wrap this up. I didn't know any current students and didn't want to get caught in a lie. "So, you didn't like his class?"

She shrugged. "He has an easy charm that keeps everyone riveted and a deep knowledge about the history of any country you throw at him, which is impressive, but for someone with a Ph.D. from Cambridge, he doesn't have a strong body of research, and there were things about his teaching style that I didn't like."

"Like what?"

She must've seen I was genuinely interested in what she had to say because she dropped her apathetic demeanor. "Well…" she thought for a moment. "I'm majoring in International Studies, which is part of the political science department, and we focus heavily on research and statistics. Chapman is part of the history department, so it might just be that his discipline has a different approach. But basically, he poses lots of hypotheticals about relationships between countries in a way that makes you feel like he's trying to get you to think outside the box, and it leads to lively discussions students love, but the wording of his hypotheticals guides students to predetermined answers. Does that make sense?"

"I need to think about it some more," I answered honestly. "But I think it does." I took my leave and went back to Anthony.

"Just in time—Pappa needs me back at the funeral home at five. We have a body to pick up in Trotwood. We can swing by the soccer field and talk to Ronnie's coach and team if we hurry."

"A body? Not another murder, I hope?"

The corner of his mouth lifted. "No, thank God. We have all we can handle." He hit reverse and pulled out. "No—a man named

Lester Reynolds. Ninety-six years old, he died at home in his sleep, and one of his last wishes was to use our funeral home. After your incident with Tessa Baker, he saw us on the news, and he said he wanted his family to hire the notorious funeral home when he died because he wanted to go out with a bang." He smiled. "His granddaughter said his sense of humor is what they will all miss most."

"I bet he had deep, expressive laugh lines," I said with a grin. "I'll do my best to make him look the way his family wants to remember him."

"You will, and in the end, that, plus Pappa's personal touch, will make us stand out from the competition." He turned right, and we left Wright State. "What did you learn?"

"Professor Van Chapman, Department of History, British accent, Ph.D. from Cambridge." I pulled out my phone to learn more about him as I spoke. "One of the girls took global studies with him and wasn't too impressed with his methods, even though he's charming and seems to keep students riveted." I typed the professor's name into my phone and repeated what the second girl had told me about him.

"Hm," I said after a while. "There isn't a lot of information on him, which I guess makes sense if he doesn't focus on research. His page on Wright State says, *Born and raised in London, Professor Chapman is a historian with a particular interest in the Western world's cultural, social, religious, and political histories. After secondary school in London, he studied history at Cambridge, staying on for an MPhil and a Ph.D. He is now a Professor of Modern History at Wright State and is co-editor of the peer-reviewed journal Historical Documents on Early Modern European Politics. He spends his free time on hiking trips around the world.* Below that, it says he has taught The West and The World since 1500, Studies in British History, Studies in Early Modern Europe,

Studies in Modern Europe, and Global Encounters. They're all undergraduate courses." I looked at Anthony. "I don't know how it all fits into it all, except maybe he was interested in my dad's research into the Fountain of Youth?"

Anthony narrowed his eyes in thought as he wove through traffic. We weren't far from the soccer fields. "So far, we know he's a modern history professor who likes to lead his students to answers instead of encouraging them to think, he travels the world, he was smirking at Lillian and Neal at their tenth-anniversary party, and that he left Performance Place about ten minutes after Lillian, who was there in a car she likely uses when she wants to fly under the radar." He shook his head. "I don't know how it all ties in, but you could be right about your dad's research. We can speculate all day long, though, and it could still be a coincidence that he and Lillian were at Performance Place at the same time. For all we know, Professor Chapman might have even been someone's plus one at Lillian and Neal's anniversary, and they don't know each other at all. I think our best bet is to question the doorman at Performance Place without arousing his suspicions. If it turns out Lillian and Professor Chapman have indeed been meeting, then at least that's a clear link between them."

I nodded and went back to scroll through search results on Professor Chapman. A few minutes later, at a red light, Anthony turned to me. "What's odd?"

"What do you mean what's odd?"

"You're biting your lip and narrowing your eyes at your phone. You don't have to be a sculptor to know you found something odd."

That got a chuckle out of me, which lightened my mood. "Well, you're right. I started reading reviews on him on websites that rate professors. Ridiculously enough, many posts are about how handsome and charming he is. He's also not known as a tough grader. But two posts stand out. One says that the student once commented about a certain country, which the student doesn't name, and the professor's whole demeanor changed. He mocked the student's answer in a way that didn't refute what they'd said but merely pointed to other countries that did the same." I looked at Anthony again to see what he thought about that.

He shrugged. "I wish they'd included more details. Professor Pretty's British. Maybe the student made a critical comment about his home country?"

I kept scrolling and reading. Many mentions of his charm and presence, and overall friendliness, until… "This one's from about eleven years ago. It claims that Professor Chapman would fish for information about his students' backgrounds during class. It was subtle and always related to the material they were discussing but that it became clear to the commenter because Chapman turned his charm on a student with high-level connections." I looked over at Anthony. "It's only one comment, but what do you think? Does it fit in with what we were saying about possible spies? Am I grasping at straws?"

Anthony shook his head as if he didn't know what to think. "Maybe. Let's file it away."

I reread the comment. "If Lillian is a *femme fatale*, then maybe Professor Pretty is a *homme fatale*. We never hear about those. All the scorn is for women. They could even be a spy team of co-*fatales*."

"It sounds straight off one of those telenovelas you say you and your Abuela love."

"They do say life imitates art," I reminded him.

Anthony let out a breath of laughter. "I'm not sure I would call a telenovela art."

I raised an eyebrow at him. "Tell that to Abuela's sister, my semi-evil Tía Josefa."

"What will she do? Hex me?"

"Worse, she'll perform a fufú."

"I thought your family only used magic for good."

"I forgot about my semi-evil Tía Josefa—I've only met her twice. The only thing she and Abuela have in common is their love for telenovelas."

"What has she done that is so *semi*-evil?"

"Her fufú power is that she can talk to anything that resembles a door and command it to open and close. When I was little, she was at a family reunion and got angry, so she locked us all in the house for three days, keeping the outer doors shut and constantly slamming all the interior doors, cabinets, and drawers. I stayed with Abuela for a long weekend holiday, and I didn't believe in magic back then, so she let me think it was all a game." I spied the soccer fields ahead, and Anthony hit the left turn signal.

"Why didn't your family call the police?"

"They did, but when the police arrived, Tía Josefa kept their car doors shut. One tried to leave through her window, but Tía commanded the car door to open as she did so, so she tumbled out. And then Tía almost shut it closed on her hand. Either way, the policewomen couldn't open the front door, and Tia denied she was doing anything, and no one could prove that she was. The police thought it was all a hoax, and they threatened to file charges if we wasted their time again."

Anthony pressed his lips together as he parked. "How did you get out?" he managed to ask, though he was holding back laughter.

I turned my most withering glare his way. "As I said, she's only semi-evil. We ran out of food, and so she let us out. Now, do you have a plan for talking to the team? I wish I had one, but there hasn't been time."

Anthony blew out a breath. "Tell me about it. Everything's been moving so fast." He shook his head. "I say we approach Sheldon since we know what he looks like because of Anne's pictures, introduce ourselves, explain that Anne asked us to look into her son's death, ask if he knows about Dan's murder yesterday, and see if he'll answer the same questions we asked Luke."

I thought about that. "How about we simply ask him if he has any insight into it?"

A pause, and then, "Let's try that. And you do the talking at first. You have a way of disarming people." He glanced at his watch. "Start by telling him it'll only take ten minutes. That's all we have."

I glowed at the compliment as we made our way to the field. Sheldon was easy to spot; he had longish hair, a lean, muscular build… and his shirt had "Coach" written across the back. There were people in the stands watching, and nobody paid us any mind until we walked right up to Sheldon. He shot us a glance and then a frown but, in the next moment, became distracted by a player who'd displayed some fancy footwork to take the ball from another player. He clapped at the first player and yelled something at the second, and I marveled at our nerve. Anthony and I exchanged a look and stepped back. It was likely we wouldn't get anywhere with the team, and it was time to let this go unless the sheriff's department became stuck.

Anthony shrugged and tapped at his watch as if to say, *let's just wait a few minutes.* A soccer ball rolled to my feet, and I stared at it for a moment. A bright green lightbulb switched on in my brain, and the memory of my fluorescent toe swam before me, filling me with excitement. Not thinking, I pulled my foot back and kicked at the ball with all my might, wondering if maybe that toe had superhuman strength. I must have been expecting the ball to fly across the field because it surprised me when my toe caught on the ground, and I tripped over the ball.

A whistle blew, and soon, both Anthony and Sheldon were helping me up. "Are you okay?" they asked simultaneously. A few players made their way to us. I tested my foot and said I was fine, but I could feel my face burning. Sheldon pointed toward the bleachers. "You're not supposed to be this close to the field. Get back."

"In a moment," Anthony said, loud enough for his voice to carry to the field and bleachers. "We only need five minutes of your time. Anne Martin asked us to help her find out what happened to her son, Ronnie, and we'd like to hear any insights you might have into the matter."

For half a second, the field went quiet, almost as if someone had hit pause. An instant later, players and spectators were closing in, talking over each other. Mostly they wanted to find out if what they had heard about Dan Martin being murdered last night was true. I gave Anthony a conspiratorial smile because I saw what he had done there. Of course, they had heard about Dan Martin, and of course, it was uppermost on their minds, practice or not. Coach Sheldon threw up his hands and sighed.

Nobody asked us who we were or why Anne Martin had asked us to help. They were eager to work through everything going through their minds for the last few days.

We answered their questions and then threw out two of our own. "Do any of you have any thoughts on Dan and Ronnie's relationship?" In response, I got different versions of what Luke had told us. Dan only came to championship games and seemed more intent on getting attention for being a locally well-known sportswriter than watching the game. He never expressed pride in Ronnie, but he took credit for developing his talent. The word narcissist was tossed out. On the other hand, Anne was at every game, cheering him on, and often invited the players out for meals, content to sit back and watch them all enjoying themselves.

Anthony's question, "Did Ronnie seem different in the weeks leading up to his death?" yielded a resounding "yes." Sheldon gave the most thoughtful response, and it was clear Ronnie had been on his mind a lot. "He wasn't putting in the same effort and seemed tired all the time. I wish that I had asked him what was going on, but I was shortsighted. I was upset with him because I thought it had to do with his upcoming transfer." He shook his head and stared at the ground. "I've been trained to spot signs of depression and burnout, but I ignored all the signs, thinking instead that he was flaking because he was moving up and leaving us behind…"

Clearly, Sheldon felt that Ronnie had taken his own life and that, as his coach, he should have noticed something was deeply wrong. His players rallied around him. I hoped that talking about it would prove cathartic to all.

Anthony tapped on his watch again, and we thanked them and took our leave after giving them one of Anthony's old business cards, instructing them to call if they thought of anything else.

A thoughtful silence settled between us as we made our way back to the funeral home. We hadn't learned anything new, but we witnessed disbelief and confusion again. I wished I could have faith that it would all be solved soon...

Lately, it had become popular to say that closure was overrated. I disagreed. We could learn to live without it when it was beyond our ability to attain it, but it didn't mean you ever stopped yearning for it...

"Why did you kick that soccer ball?" Anthony asked, interrupting my thoughts.

I looked over at him, surprised I hadn't yet told him about my third ear, green left toe, and Mahoney's crest. Things were moving so fast...

A brief explanation later, I was at the receiving end of a disappointed look. "You're sure you didn't see any fluorescent green on me when I picked you up after the, uh, ceremony?" he asked.

I shook my head. "Not that I could see."

"So unfair." He frowned. "And now, on top of everything else, we need to figure out if your green toe is your Achilles' heel. Or what power it has. And whatever the heck Mahoney's crest is."

We were crossing the Main Street bridge then, and the flash of multiple police lights in the funeral home parking lot made all other thoughts disappear. "Pappa!" I exclaimed.

Anthony pressed down hard on the gas, and we soon sped into the driveway, where we joined two sheriff's cars, the Montgomery County coroner's van, and a large black pick-up.

Inside the embalming room, we were met by two deputies along with Lieutenant Mahoney and Sergeant Beemer. Anne was also there, biting her lip as she followed the technician's movements. She avoided looking at Ronnie's body, which was covered by a white blanket. We sidled up to Pappa, who leaned over to whisper, "They're taking Ronnie's body to the county coroner's office."

Anthony's eyes widened. "So, they suspect he was murdered, too." He then walked over to Anne, who was also there, holding herself tense with an iron grip on her phone. "Hello, Mrs Martin. I was so sorry to hear about what happened last night," he said, hitting just the right note.

Anne nodded jerkily. "Montgomery County has taken over Ronnie's case now, too. They're taking him to the coroner for further tests or evidence gathering…" She closed her eyes. "I just want this nightmare to be over with. I don't know which way is up anymore." When she opened her eyes, she glanced at her phone, and I got the impression that she was expecting an important call or text.

Soon, the transfer was complete. Everyone was outside, watching the van leave. It felt like we were sending our hopes for justice and resolution with Ronnie.

Anthony went over to speak to Mahoney, and I eyed them warily. Mahoney pinned me with a look I couldn't quite interpret. They were talking about me.

Pappa caught my eye and pointed to his watch. "We should be back in about two hours." He and Anthony left for Trotwood to pick up Lester Reynolds, and Mahoney gently asked Anne if she was up for some more questions, but she shook her head.

"I can't. Not in my current state. When I got the call that you'd be picking up Ronnie, I didn't think. I just drove out here in my pickup. But I'm about to collapse. My therapist prescribed Xanax, and I've decided to go home and take it, so I can rest and meet you at the station later and help as much as I can."

Mahoney nodded in understanding. "I can get someone to drive you home, and we can get the pickup out to you later."

Again, Anne shook her head. "There's no need. A friend is picking me up in an Uber—I'll take the Uber home, and then they'll follow in my truck."

Feeling superfluous, I took my leave, went inside, and sank into the chair in front of the desk to try to work through all my thoughts and emotions. A lot was going on. The only way forward was to center myself and focus on one thing at a time.

Knowing both Ronnie's and Dan's last words suddenly felt like a burden. It would help solve the case, but my hands were tied. Hopefully, the sheriff's office would gather enough evidence to arrest the murderer or murderers without my interference. And if they didn't…

A long, drawn-out breath helped relieve some of my tension. There was nothing I could do but cross that bridge if it came to it. *Prioritize, Angie.* I fired up the laptop in front of me, went to the professors' rating site, and scanned the facts and questions section to see if it was possible to contact other students there.

It was—but only if the user had allowed it when they signed up. If their username was clickable, it meant they had opted in. I created an account, and a thrill ran down my spine when I saw that the username for both students with the intriguing posts about Professor Van Chapman was clickable.

I came up with what I hoped was a compelling cover story for my questions to the students. It was possible they'd never answer, especially the student who had posted the oldest comment, but it felt good to do something.

There was a knock on the door, and I clicked on the security camera app Anthony had installed. The back door view showed Anne Martin. Behind her, Mahoney was on the phone and pacing. With a shake of my head, I realized that as wary as I was of him, I wouldn't open the door to Anne if he wasn't there. Not after what happened with Tessa Baker.

I opened the door, and Anne reached forward to squeeze my arm in gratitude gently. "I want to thank you for all your help. I believe the information you and Anthony got from Luke will help solve Ronnie's case. But I also wanted to let you know that I no longer need your…detective services." She released my arm to gesture toward Mahoney.

I nodded in understanding and said, "I'm so very sorry for both your losses, Mrs. Martin."

Anne tensed and looked like she was at a loss for words. Finally, she took a shaky breath and said, "Dan's last words to me were that he wanted us to go away together, and it's all I can think about now. Getting away for a while, I mean."

At that, I froze. Dan Martin's last words to his murderer were an offer to go away together…

Could he have been speaking to Anne?

I managed not to swallow or lick my suddenly dry lips. Instead, I softened my gaze and said, "You've been through a lot. Please know we're still here for you if you need anything."

Her phone buzzed, she glanced down, and her shoulders sagged in relief. "My ride is here." With a final look of gratitude, she left.

It took all I had not to run over to Mahoney, but I wanted to wait until she was safely around the corner and up the driveway. Finally, I beckoned him over with a furious wave of my hand. "Come inside! We need to talk!"

He put his palms out in front of him as he stepped closer. "I'm still here because Anthony asked me to stay with you, so don't start complaining about me being in your soup again—*nobody* gets what that means."

When he was close enough, I pulled him inside and shut the door. "No—I think Anne is the murderer! You need to go after her!"

He straightened and got a new look in his eye. "Why do you think Anne is the murderer?"

And like an idiot, I stood there, staring at him. How could I tell him that I suspected Anne was the murderer because she had repeated Dan's last words? How would I explain that I knew what Dan's last words were? I went through various scenarios in my head, like that I had heard Dan the previous night, just before he died, but then why wouldn't I have told the police about that last night? I shook my head. *"You need to trust me."*

"Based on what?" He placed his hands on my shoulders when I didn't answer and searched my eyes. "I don't understand you, Angie, but I want to trust you. Come on. Give me a reason."

I looked into his eyes and tried to think. "Because…because…."
There was nothing for it. The truth. "I have reason to believe she
was with him last night *right* before he was stabbed—oof." The
door to the stairs that led to the hall outside Pappa's office flew
open, and I was thrown against Mahoney. He caught me, but
before I could turn to see who had joined us, I heard a blowing
sound, and then a sweet scent enveloped us. Mahoney blinked
and began to cough. I turned, a hand clamped down over my
eyes, and a sweet-smelling petal was stuffed under my nose.

TWELVE

I t was as if a mere thread bound my soul and body together.
The former drifted above, unconcerned, the latter pooled
uncomfortably on a hard surface. Vaguely I remembered
receiving quiet instructions, a car, a stumbling walk, and then
drifting off.

After a while, the thread grew taut, and my soul began to float
down to meet my body. With effort, I got up on one elbow. I
blinked when I realized I was behind an ornate iron gate, looking
out onto grass and tombstones. "Am I dead?" I croaked,
wondering if the rumored pearly gates were instead made of
metal.

"Angie?" A male voice rasped. I turned my fuzzy head toward it.
Lieutenant Brian Mahoney was also here, struggling to push
himself up to a sitting position against a marble wall. "Are you
okay?" he asked.

My throat was parched and dry and felt aflame. "I think so," was all I could manage as I hauled myself up enough to lean against the cool wall beside him.

"I'm so sorry," a whispered voice called on the other side of the gates. As my eyes adjusted to the darkness, I made out a tall figure with a pair of hands half-covering its face. "I used devil's breath on you both. Not much. Only enough to have you quietly follow me to my car and then walk here before you became semi-unconscious."

"Where are we?" Mahoney asked in a thick voice.

"Locked in the mausoleum at the back of the cemetery. I parked on a side street and walked you here, then stuck around to make sure you'd be okay and explain." The nervous voice was male and somewhat familiar, but he moved back, and I couldn't see his face.

It hurt to swallow, but I managed to wet my throat enough to ask, "Who are you?"

Hesitation. "I need to leave soon, but I'll pass you some saddlebags with water and groats. You should be able to shout for help in a few hours."

"Groats," Mahoney repeated.

"Oats without hulls. They're meant for horses, but they're suitable for human consumption. It's all Mrs. Martin had in her truck."

I touched my hand to my forehead and tried to think through the throbbing pain and dizziness. Horse feed. Suitable for human consumption. Anne Martin was a veterinarian. It all came back to me then—that she knew Dan Martin's last words and must have been there when he died. But I couldn't get the words out.

The man began to pace, and I finally caught a glimpse of his face. It gave me a jolt of adrenaline, enough to say, "Luke," and "murderer!"

Luke walked forward and hung onto the gates. "No! I'm *not* a murderer. It was an accident. I was saving Anne. But no one will believe it. And she can barely think straight, but she's about to crack. I know it." He looked at me. "And I heard you talking to Mahoney. Somehow, you know she was there. I don't know how you know, but you do." I tried to follow his rant and agitated pacing, but it made my head spin, and I nearly heaved.

Mahoney managed to stand up and take two steps before falling onto his knees. "Water," he repeated in a desperate voice.

Luke spun around a few times before finally locating the promised saddlebags. He shoved them between the iron bars, promising, "You'll be okay. I just need time to get away. I have a plan."

We fumbled with the saddlebags until Mahoney dragged out a bottle of water. He opened it and handed it to me. As much as I wanted to gulp it all down, I took a long, alleviating sip and gave it back to him since he seemed to lack the strength to open another. The gulps wetted his throat enough for him to say, "You're obstructing a murder investigation, and you've poisoned and kidnapped two people, one of them a federal officer. But I can help you. Turn yourself in before you get into more trouble." But the gulps and effort at speech had been too much because he doubled over and began coughing and heaving.

Something in Mahoney's short speech stood out to me, but when I tried to think it through, it scrambled away as if hiding from the pain of thought.

A movement from Luke made me look over at him. It seemed like he didn't know whether to stay or leave or what to do, and a semblance of sense began to break through the haze. He had said something about it all being an accident. And he'd stayed because he wasn't sure we'd be all right. I found another water bottle and sipped at it slowly as Mahoney leaned back against the marble again. His breaths were shallow now and uneven. I wiped my mouth and turned to Luke. Desperately I tried to think up a plan, but my brain felt too tired to work that hard. "I believe you're not a murderer, but you need to explain it all to us, please, so we can help." It was the truth and all I could think of to say.

Luke stared at me a long moment before transferring his gaze to Mahoney. "How about you? Do you want the truth, or do you only care about closing the investigation?"

Beside me, Mahoney took another swig of water before saying. "I'm not motivated by stats. I'm motivated by fairness." It sounded as if his brain was also too tired to elaborate.

Scoffing softly, Luke said, "I'll tell you what happened. I planned to, anyway. But I'm hiding out while you investigate it. I've seen and heard too much to put my life in another's hands." He shook his head as if hardly believing he was in the current situation, but he began to talk after taking a deep breath.

"Shortly after Angie and Anthony Pappalardo questioned me, Mrs. Martin came by and asked if she could start packing up Ronnie's stuff. I stayed in the living room instead of offering to help because I felt guilty that I had told you about the letter to Tender Tim when I hadn't told her. After a while, I took the letter into the room to show it to her and found her sitting on the bed, looking shellshocked.

"She told me that before coming over, she had gone on a long walk in the woods behind her house to try to make sense of what had happened to Ronnie and that she had spotted a poisonous nightshade planted on the side of a ravine, deep in the woods. She recognized it because a pony had gotten poisoned by it out in Wyoming when she trained there. I didn't know why she was telling me this and figured she was in shock and simply babbling, but then she asked me if there had been a strong flowery scent in the room the night I found Ronnie. I told her yes.

"She pulled a baggie with a yellow petal from her purse and asked me to take a quick whiff and tell her if it was the same scent. She was crying, and I thought she was having a breakdown and I wondered if I should call an ambulance. But I agreed to smell the flower while I figured out what to do."

Luke paused then. "It was the same scent. Strong and sweet. Then she pulled the baggie away, sealed it, and explained what happens if a person sniffs too much." He looked at us steadily. "They lose their free will. They become zombie-like. And highly manipulable."

"Devil's breath," Mahoney said the words I'd been thinking, and we looked at each other, having both just been subjected to its powers.

Luke gave us a solemn nod. "She said she had told Dan about the flower years ago. I looked it up on my phone, thinking that she was grasping at straws, but I saw that it was real. I handed the letter over to her, telling everything I'd told you, about me being Tender Tim, and about Ronnie's reaction when he read the letter. And she knew. She had no doubt. Dan had killed Ronnie.

"I told her we should call the police, that we now had more evidence than a simple gut feeling, but she was adamant that nobody would listen. And the more we talked it over, the more I had to agree. We couldn't prove that Dan had written the letter to Tender Tim. We couldn't prove that the deadly nightshade had ever been in the room or had even been planted by Dan in the woods behind her house. An investigator or reporter with resources might be able to prove it, but we didn't have anything substantial enough for anyone to open an investigation."

Frustration laced his words, and I wanted to believe that Luke was wrong. That someone would have listened. But when I turned to Mahoney to seek reassurance, his eyes revealed the truth. Luke was right. It wasn't enough. "What did you do?" I asked.

"They came up with their own plan," Mahoney replied.

Luke held up two fingers. "We came up with two plans. If the first failed, Anne would hire a private investigator. But we felt time was of the essence, so we staged a scene in Dan's office to let him know that someone was on to him, and we planted one of those discreet nanny cams to catch him if he let anything slip. And we were both recording, but at a safe distance because we knew he was dangerous. We weren't foolish enough to think we could get a confession, but we planned to surprise him enough so that he would reveal something, in either words or actions. I was outside the sliding glass door, and Anne was inside the master bedroom, directly in front of Dan's study. But it all went wrong." Shaken, Luke closed his eyes for a long time, and I wasn't sure we'd ever hear the rest.

Every time I spoke, my throat felt as if it grew thicker, no matter how much water I drank, and I wanted to save my words. "I believe you," I said after a while. "But how did it all go wrong?"

Luke opened his eyes and seemed far away. "Dan played it cool. He took one look around and immediately summed up what was happening. He didn't even blink, not even at the poisonous flowers we thought for sure he would rush to throw out of the room. And he guessed Anne was behind it all. He flipped the script and started talking as if he knew Anne had killed Ronnie and that the staged scene was real, and she was about to kill him, too. But Anne apparently couldn't take it anymore because she ran into the study and started yelling at him between sobs, letting all her feelings out, accusing him of killing Ronnie and never having loved him, of being a narcissist, you name it.

"I looked in and watched as Dan sat down at his desk. He barely took his eyes off Anne as he opened the bottom drawer and thumbed through to a file, which Anne now believes was the will. We think he was making sure it was still there and that we hadn't found it. Stupidly, we didn't even think to look for a motive other than him finding out that Ronnie wasn't his son."

Luke shook his head, and his voice grew shaky. "And then he opened the top drawer and slowly drew out a gun. He cocked it. Anne was hysterical and didn't notice. He continued his ruse, telling her he knew she was the killer but that he would forgive her, and they could go away together. But I think the scent of the flowers was affecting him because he swayed. When he steadied himself, he quickly raised the gun and pointed it at her, she screamed, and I stopped thinking. There was a letter opener on the desk..." Luke's breathing became shaky. "And—and I grabbed it... and..." He couldn't say the words.

"And then you and Pappa arrived." He turned to me, tears streaming down his face. "And I didn't know what to do. I grabbed the nanny cam. But the flowers were starting to influence Anne, too, because she could barely move but let me drag her along through the woods to my car. She just now told me she wants us to confess everything, but I prefer to hide away while she sorts it out. I've had time to think, and I decided to write a true-crime book about it and get my side of the story out in case we can't prove what happened and to have some income since I know I've lost the Tender Tim column forever now. And I think it'll be cathartic." His voice cracked. "I never meant to kill him. I only meant to stop him from killing Anne." Then he wiped his tears and face with his sleeve and said, "You'll be okay. And maybe, we'll all be okay," and walked away.

Mahoney was still hoarse, but he tried, in vain, to shout after him. With a breath of frustration, he dropped down next to me again. I grabbed two more bottles of water. "Drink and save your breath and energy. We should try to scream and shout for help as soon as possible."

He agreed, slowly drank up, and leaned back to rest. I wondered if anyone was looking for us and what Luke had done with our phones. If Anthony missed me and looked at security footage, what would he see?

A glance at Mahoney's watch told me it was only eleven at night. "Or maybe we should try to scream now, before it's too late for anyone to hear us," I reconsidered. But after several attempts, we realized neither of us could project our voices more than a few yards.

I tried to wrap my brain around everything that had happened but couldn't manage complicated thinking. After a while, my eyes grew heavy, and I began to shiver. My head felt cold, too, and I wanted to understand if anything I was feeling was normal, if it was withdrawal, or if I would suffer permanent damage from the Devil's Breath. Mahoney bucked, and I realized he was shaking, too. He pulled me in front of him, and I turned into his chest, taking comfort in his arms, warmth, and scent. *Irish Spring and sweetness*, I thought as I closed my eyes.

When I opened them again, the moon was high in a cloudless sky, my mouth felt like it was stuffed with cotton, my thirst bordered on desperation, and at some point, my arms had crept around Mahoney's neck. "You can stay," he murmured when I began to disentangle myself, and his breath made me shiver again. "You fit. Like a piece of a puzzle."

The scattered pieces of my brain had begun to settle into place, enough to know his words impacted me, but I could not follow my thoughts and feelings from beginning to end. "Neither of us is acting normally. Do you think we'll stay like this forever?"

Mahoney cleared his throat to try to get it to work, and I handed him my water. "I researched devil's breath yesterday," he explained after taking a swig. "And it seems like we're out of the toxic phase, but the scopolamine inhibits higher brain function for hours."

"You must be doing great if you can remember all that."

He stretched out a leg. "No. For my life, I can't think of a way to get us out of here. I can't plan. It's why scopolamine has also been used as a sort of truth serum. Lies require a complicated thought process, too."

A small alarm went off in my head. Not because I *wanted* to lie, but it wasn't good that I couldn't. There were secrets… "I haven't even been trying to think of a plan. At least you have," I said, to keep my currently truth-telling mind away from my secrets.

"When was the last time you ate?" Mahoney suddenly asked.

"Noon."

"Here. I always carry butterscotch in my pocket. I don't know if sucking on them can keep hunger at bay, but it might help with our throats." He was right, they helped with my throat.

I smiled. "It's cute that you carry butterscotch in your pocket."

"I'm an Eagle Scout."

"That doesn't surprise me." I laughed into his chest, and he hugged me closer. "We are so different," I said softly.

"Yes, you wear loud, glittery blue toenail polish, and I don't," he joked as he looked down at my toenails, but he sighed when he saw I was serious. "I've led a charmed life. I know that. But it doesn't mean I don't feel for others. I care deeply about what happened to your parents and how life as you knew it was stolen from you. I want you to get justice, whatever that means for you, and I hate that you don't believe me." It was said quietly, whispered into my hair. There was no defensiveness in his tone. He wasn't trying to convince me. He was stating his simple truth.

"Are you ready to try screaming again?" I asked because I couldn't handle the complicated feelings blooming in my chest. He agreed, and for a while, we took turns until we realized we were shouting out into nothingness. The mausoleum was too far back for anyone to hear us. Not even Anthony at the carriage house. Scurrying sounds were our only company. "Are those mice?"

"Rats."

"Rats!" I sat up.

"At least we won't starve," he teased.

"I will. But at least I'll die in a mausoleum. You can just leave me here. And my epitaph can read, here lies Angie Gomez Gomez, a young woman whose selflessness, coupled with high culinary standards, led her to sacrifice herself so Lieutenant Brian Mahoney could live off rats."

He chuckled. "If you can dictate your epitaph to me, your brain function must be more advanced than mine."

I smiled because my head did feel clearer. Enough so that a moment later, a new sound filled the air and brought back a recent memory. "Do you hear that?"

"More rats?"

"No. A rooster," I exclaimed. "And it sounds close by. It must be here in the cemetery."

He yawned, and it must've hurt because he let go of me long enough to rub his throat. "One of my neighbors keeps a small chicken coop. Maybe they have a rooster, and it escaped."

Visuals of my grandmother's visit this morning began to flit through my mind's eye, ending in a fluorescent green crest on top of Mahoney's head. Hadn't Wanda said something about a neighbor who could speak to llamas and had only found out because the opportunity presented itself? I turned in Mahoney's arms, grabbed his shirt, and said, "You need to call the rooster over and ask it to go get help."

"Call the rooster over...?" He smoothed my hair away from my face and looked into my eyes with a troubled gaze.

I racked my brain to think of a credible way of explaining to him that I had seen a fluorescent green crest on his head and that it was possible he could communicate with roosters and that he should try to tell it to get Anthony. But my brain thought this too taxing and began putting up roadblocks again. It was difficult enough to understand, let alone explain. "Are you still manipulable?" I asked instead.

His lip quirked up in one corner. "What do you want to manipulate me into doing?"

I licked my lips. "I would really, really like you to call out to the rooster and ask it to go to the carriage house and make enough of a ruckus to wake up Anthony. Maybe if Anthony opens his window and we try to shout again, he'll hear us."

He stared at my lips before slowly lifting his gaze to mine. "Is licking your lips part of your ploy to manipulate me?"

The ability to breathe abandoned me. Without meaning to, my gaze dropped to his mouth. "N—not c—consciously," I stuttered. For many nights now, I had been fighting the memory of his kiss the night of the LOWO fundraiser. The fight left me now. The memory intruded. His lips had felt so nice. Warm and firm… I swayed toward him.

"Rooster!" Mahoney called, and my brain, now more scrambled than before, could only think that he was even slower to recover, or maybe, he didn't want to kiss me. My heart clenched painfully, and the disappointment left me confused.

I looked away, only to see the rooster amble up and regard Mahoney expectantly. Mahoney, a look of shock on his face, stared back.

I shook his arm. "Talk to it!"

"Um." Mahoney blinked. "My friend here would like you to go to that carriage house over there," he pointed. "And, uh, make a ton of noise."

"Tell it to go specifically to one of the second-story windows on the east side of the carriage house, flap its wings against it, and crow until a man looks out. Oh! And tell him to hold this in his beak. Anthony will know to follow it!" I scrambled up and took the receipt with Professor Van Chapman's tag number out of my pocket, thrilled that my brain was finally gaining higher function.

After a long, resigned look at me, he got up and repeated my instructions to our new friend while studying the piece of paper I'd handed him. "Why do you have a receipt from Advanced Spy Systems in your pocket?" he asked me. Apparently, his brain was regaining function, too, while mine couldn't have been as advanced as I'd previously thought, or else I would never have handed him evidence of our spying.

"I think it's where Anthony bought the new equipment." It was the truth. I hadn't been with Anthony when he bought the security equipment and trackers, so I couldn't be sure.

He turned it around, took a good look at the license plate number I'd written on the back, and I could practically see the wheels turning in his head. Thankfully, the wheels must've gotten stuck because he shook his head again and reluctantly stuck the receipt through the gate, looking floored when the rooster took it from his hand and waddled away.

It took a long moment for him to process that, straighten, and look back at me. "I did all that for one reason only, you know."

Confused, I could only look at him.

"To be in your good graces for once," he explained.

I smiled. "Well. That did it. I'll never forget it." The sound of police sirens intruded, but we didn't pay them much heed. Police sirens could always be heard in the city. Instead, we studied each other for a long moment.

Then, I was in his arms without conscious thought, and he was holding me as if he'd never let me go. On a desperate breath, we came together in an open-mouthed kiss that felt as if it would only satisfy us if it never ended. Our breaths and sighs mingled, and we couldn't get enough. The fever heightened, his hands crept up to the back of my head, and mine wrapped around his neck as we both fought for better access. It was fire and magic.

"Over there! The mausoleum!" came a sudden shout, and we simultaneously let out a frustrated sob at the interruption. "There's a flash of orange, and Angie Gomez Gomez was last seen wearing a fluorescent orange shirt!"

"It's hardly fluorescent," I murmured, still breathless, against Mahoney's lips, and I felt him smile before he sighed. We each took a step back, gazes locked, just as multiple flashlights found us. A growing number of voices rushed toward us, but still, we couldn't tear our eyes away from each other. Because we knew something would be lost. Then everyone was upon us, and we had no choice. "We should thank the rooster," I said, to fill the sudden void between us with something we'd never forget.

Amused, Mahoney turned to Sergeant Beemer. "How'd you find us?" he asked as she unlocked the gates.

"The Pappalardos reviewed their security footage and saw both you and Miss Gomez left with Luke Wilson in Anne Martin's pickup. They noticed you were both acting strangely, and they called me. When we couldn't reach *any* of you, we put out an APB on Wilson and the pickup and questioned Mrs. Martin before finding Luke."

"Did they confess?" I asked.

"Yes, and both she and Luke are at the station. He told us where he left you. Your cell phones were still in the pickup."

"Angie!" a voice called, and I turned toward it to see Anthony running up the path. The gate to the mausoleum was open now, and I ran through it, straight into his arms.

"We were so worried!" he said, hugging me close. "Are you okay?"

"I think so, but Luke used devil's breath on us. I'm better now, but I still feel…floaty."

He held me at arm's length, did a once over, and when he saw I was unharmed, said, "The craziest thing …" Wide-eyed, he handed me the receipt Mahoney had given to the rooster.

My eyes flew to his. "Did he flap his wings against your window?"

"No, he found me in the driveway, waddled right up, and deposited it into my hand, and I instantly knew it was from you. I followed him to the cemetery and then saw the police cars." I looked beyond Anthony to see the rooster, but the rooster was watching Mahoney. "How'd you manage to get a rooster to deliver a message?" he asked, perplexed.

"Brian Mahoney can talk to them! That's what his fluorescent green crest was about!" The rooster crowed, and the sound was so out of place that everyone, including Mahoney, swung their heads to look at it. Mahoney then lifted his gaze to mine before glancing down to the receipt in my hand. I scrunched it up, and he ambled over to us.

"How are you feeling?" Anthony asked him.

"I want nothing more than to go down to the station and talk to Luke and Anne, but I still feel out of it. I'll only get in the way."

Anthony nodded. "You should go home and sleep it off."

Mahoney agreed and gave me a look. "Angie should do the same."

I cleared my throat. "What have you learned so far?" I asked him, not fully able to look him in the eye after that kiss.

"So far, everything Luke told us check's out. The nanny cam Anne and Luke bought had a wider range than they realized, and it caught Dan Martin about to shoot a defenseless Anne. Anne Martin also gave up his computer, and an initial search already shows Dan Martin had been looking up the effects of devil's breath and suicide by hanging. They also found the letter Dan Martin wrote to Tender Tim."

Anthony let out a long whistle. "And that's only the preliminaries."

Mahoney gave him another nod but continued to look at me. "I've already said I'm not going to press kidnapping charges against Luke in a personal capacity. But they want me to wait until I'm in my right mind to decide."

"I'm not going to press charges either," I said. "No lasting harm was done, and he was under extreme duress." But the word *kidnapping* brought up a memory, and my eyes flew up to meet Mahoney's. "When you threatened to bring Luke up on kidnapping charges, you told him you were a federal officer...*federal*."

Mahoney shrugged. "I was not of sound mind." With that, he turned and left.

Anthony and I stared at each other. "With everything we now know, that brings up interesting possibilities, especially when his brother is the district attorney," he said, but before he could elaborate, we caught Pappa limping up the cemetery walkway, with Abuela patiently walking alongside him.

"Angie!" They cried in relief, and I raced down to reassure them that I had emerged unscathed from my latest adventure, even though I was eager to hear the rest of Anthony's thoughts.

Abuela, Pappa, and Tito were all caught up by the time we were in the carriage house. Abuela tried to wrap her head around it all. "So, when Dan Martin found out Ronnie wasn't his son, he cooked up a plot to murder him and make it look like a suicide so he could get a hold of the trust money that Anne would inherit. Anne was a light sleeper and never felt Dan leave that night, so she didn't suspect him until she found the devil's breath in their woods and found a petal in Ronnie's room. And then Luke showed her the letter, and she knew. But since no one had believed that Ronnie had been murdered in the first place, she and Luke decided to stage a scene and try to get Dan to confess somehow. Instead, he turned the tables on her and almost killed her. And in between, old family secrets were revealed." She shook her head. "That's always the case."

I nodded yes, and then nodded off. Unfortunately, Abuela was not about to let me sleep in cemetery dirt-filled clothes. She said it would bring me bad juju.

After a hot shower (with eucalyptus soap Abuela happened to have on her) and a change of clothes, Pappa and Abuela each gave me a comforting bear-hug goodbye. I zombie-walked to my room, but Anthony stopped me before Tito, and I could dive headfirst onto my bed. He held up the round, melted candle blob from this morning and grinned. "Is this the remnant of the cojoba candle?"

I stared at it, and for a wild moment, I didn't see the remains of a melted candle. In my mind's eye, I saw my dad's amber pendant. "Yes," I said uncertainly as details of the last few days flashed in my mind, trying to tell me something. *Cojoba. Devil's breath. Plants. Powerful effects.* A new thought began winding its way into my mind, but I was too tired to let it reach its destination. All I could do was dissolve onto my bed as one of my mother's favorite Don Quixote quotes fluttered among my sleepy thoughts. "Tomorrow is a new day. To withdraw is not to run away… It is the part of a wise man to keep himself today for tomorrow." And I needed to keep myself for tomorrow if I was ever going to solve my parents' murders.

WORDS WITH FRIENDS

ANGIE GOMEZ COZY MURDER MYSTERY, BOOK 3

Knock… KNOCK.., *KNOCK,*

Silence.

KNOCK! Bang. BANG. *BANG!*

"Anthony!" I shouted before cradling my head with both hands. I glanced at the clock. It was 10 AM.

Tomorrow was here.

I sprang up, but the abrupt action made me grab hold of my churning stomach. For a moment, I thought maybe I was hungover, which didn't make sense because I hadn't had a drink since Abuela made her famous Coquito at Christmas. Then I remembered—Devil's breath. Luke kidnaped Mahoney and me. The kiss. Luke's confession that he and Anne accidentally killed Dan Martin. New suspicions about my dad's amber pendant…

Anthony stuck his head through the half-open door. "It's Nalissa," he said with disdain. "I doubt you're in any condition to deal with her, and I'll bet all she wants is the latest scoop."

"I hear you, Anthony!" Nalissa yelled through the front door. "And believe me, you'll want to hear this."

Anthony gave me a look that said, should we believe her? I sighed and held my hand out so he could haul me up and out of bed. "Hold her off while I change, wash my face with cold water, and brush my teeth," I instructed.

Minutes later, I walked into the living room to see that Anthony had yet to let her in. They were still negotiating terms through the door. "Both Ronnie and Dan's murders are essentially solved. That's all you're getting until you give us something in return," he said.

"I already know that Dan killed Ronnie, and Luke stabbed Dan to defend Anne when they confronted him. And I know Luke used devil's breath to render Angie and Mahoney helpless when he got spooked that Angie had figured it all out and was telling Mahoney," she recited, managing to sound superior even through the closed door. "I have a better source than you will ever be inside the department. That's why I'm here, dunderhead. Because of my excellent source, I have information for you!"

I was impressed, but Anthony merely crossed his arms over his chest. "You may know the essential details, but you don't have a first-hand account or quotes from Angie and me about the ordeal."

"Why would I want a quote from you?" she asked. I shook my head, wondering how long I should let the stalemate continue. It was like dealing with children.

"It's because of me that she and Mahoney were found. See?" Anthony shot a smug look at the door. "You don't know everything."

I was about to negotiate a truce, but Nalissa seemed to have finally had enough because she shouted, "Craig and Jessica Fisher are dead!"

———

Available in Paperback and eBook from Your Favorite Bookstore or Online Retailer

ABOUT THE AUTHOR

Ines Saint was born in Zaragoza, Spain and grew up with one foot on an island of Puerto Rico and the other in the States. She's bilingual and bicultural and has spent the last eighteen years raising her fun, inspiring boys and sharing her life with her husband/best friend/biggest fan. Her greatest joys are spending quality time with family and close friends, traveling, reading feel-good historical fiction, hiking, and snuggling next to her dog, Hobbit.

www.inessaint.com

 twitter.com/Ines_Saint
instagram.com/InesSaintBooks